THE HUNGA

JILL BARRY

Copyright © 2022 Jill Barry

All rights reserved. No part of this publication may be reproduced, distributed, or transmitted in any form or by any means, without prior written permission.

This is a work of fiction. Names, characters, places, and incidents are a product of the author's imagination. Places and public names are sometimes used for atmospheric purposes. Any resemblance to anyone, living or dead, or to businesses, companies, events, institutions, or localities is completely coincidental.

ISBN: 9798351308999

With many thanks for all your expertise and support and for putting up with the author's foibles: Paul Burridge of publishingbuddy.co.uk for the cover design and layout, Dawn Kentish Knox Author and Friend, Thomas Stanniland – a refreshingly youthful member of the team keeping the author on her toes.

CHAPTER 1

"Listen to that screaming, Kay!" The evening breeze ruffling Bonnie's golden hair, made her push a strand away from her face. "You'd think people were being thrown off the cliffs."

Her friend laughed. "We're exactly the same when we ride the big dipper. You get to the top of that first steep slope and kind of hover ..."

"Before plunging to your doom. Mwah hah hah!" Bonnie linked arms with her friend. "Well, will it be the scenic railway for us tonight? Or do we choose two of the smaller rides like we did last week?"

The evening was still warm and sunny. Beyond the golden sands which gave the town its name and attracted so many visitors, the channel of water dividing Wales from England appeared calm and sparkly. The Victorian pier jutting out in the distance was attracting people seeking tranquillity away from the screams and loud music blaring from the Fun Fair.

"Or, we could take a walk on the pier and have an ice-cream in the café at the end?" Bonnie suggested.

"Are you pulling my leg? That's for young lovers and old married couples, holding hands while they watch the sunset." Kay pointed to a pleasure steamer chugging towards the pier, its white funnels gleaming, its paddles churning more slowly as the captain eased the vessel in, allowing passengers to disembark. Some day trippers were leaning on the rail, some waving to people on the pier.

"There's the *Ravenswood* coming in and my dad's working on it today. Let's keep away from the pier, if you don't mind. If he noticed us, he'd be sure to tell me I'm wearing too much make up or my skirt's too short. You'd think we were in 1857, instead of 1957! You don't know how lucky you are."

At once Kay stopped walking and clamped her hand to her mouth, her eyes showing dismay as she looked at her friend.

"Don't worry, Kay. You know I can barely remember my dad. He always used to be away at sea for months at a time, don't forget. He's been gone for ten years now, but I bet if he was with us, he'd be just the same as your dad is. You should remember your father's only looking out for you. Ever since 1947, my poor mother has had to be two parents rolled into one."

"It must've been awful for her being told her husband was lost at sea. If it's any consolation, my parents think your mum's done a brilliant job of bringing you up."

"Really?" Bonnie felt a warm glow. "That's nice of them. Come on then, let's wander round before we decide what to spend our money on."

The girls walked along the promenade and crossed the road towards the wrought-iron archway bearing the sign *Pleasure Park.* Children's merry-go-rounds, swing boats and a child-friendly helter-skelter were grouped together, the most popular ride being a roundabout crammed with miniature vehicles. A green tractor and a shiny red fire engine with silver handles and googly-eyed headlights stood either side of a police car. But all remained at a standstill now most parents had taken their little ones home, or back to their holiday bed and breakfasts.

Bonnie breathed in the familiar aroma of fried onions rising from the hot dog stall. Further on, sideshows and stands lined the righthand side of the amusements area. To the left lay the huge bulk of the scenic railway, dominating the fairground. Every so often, high above them, a car would clatter along the track, its screaming passengers hanging on for dear life to the safety rail fastening them in.

Kay darted over to the coconut shy, where she'd spotted somebody she knew. Bonnie stood watching the dignified rise and fall of the painted horses on the biggest carousel on the park as the ride moved round and round. She'd loved to ride this roundabout once she outgrew the children's attractions. The hurdy-gurdy pumped out *The Farmer Needs a Wife* while a few yards away, Elvis Presley belted out *Jailhouse Rock*.

Bonnie, backing away as a group of lads with linked arms barged through the concourse, bumped into someone behind her and whirled round immediately.

"Oh! I'm so sorry." She was staring up at a dark-haired young man. And he was gazing back at her, a strange expression on his face.

"Um, I didn't mean to tread on your toes ..." She felt oddly breathless. The stranger's dark brown eyes were mesmerising.

"It is good. No harm done. Those boys were drunk and were not political!"

She couldn't help smiling. "Yes, they'd certainly forgotten their manners. I'm glad I didn't hurt you."

"I cannot think you would ever hurt any peoples, Miss."

Later, Bonnie would remember thinking she wished she could stand there forever, gazing into the handsome stranger's beautiful brown eyes. But Kay had other ideas.

"Bonnie!" her friend called. "Come and say hello to Jack. I haven't seen him for ages and now here he is, working on the Wall of Death."

"Your name is Bonnie?"

"That's me."

A wide smile suddenly lit up the stranger's solemn countenance. He held out his hand. "Patrik Matyaz. I have to get back to work now. You come to Spanish Waltzer maybe?"

She nodded, suddenly breathless. Suddenly and puzzlingly filled with joy. "I'll come soon. Me and my friend." Why had she lost control of her speech? Her thoughts were spinning like the cars she could see twirling and tumbling on the Waltzer.

He nodded. Gave her a half-salute. "It is good."

Bonnie watched him weave his way through the crowd of holidaymakers. Although most of the townsfolk avoided the pleasure park during the peak season, there were always teenagers around, plus day trippers arriving mainly by train and coach. As if through a dense mist, she heard Kay call her name again, and pulling herself together, Bonnie walked over to join her friend and Jack and tried to concentrate on what they were saying.

"Who was that boy you were talking to? Shall we queue for the big dipper?" Kay's gaze remained on the back view of Jack, trim in dark blue dungarees as he headed back to work. "I never knew he had a job here, but you and I have never taken any notice of the lads working on the Wall of Death, have we?"

"So many questions!" Bonnie shook her head in despair. "I don't remember you going out with anyone called Jack."

"That's because you were doing your A Levels. You were always at the library with your head in a book back then. Anyway, he didn't last long." Her eyes narrowed. "He seems to have changed a lot since I saw him last, though. He just told me he wants to see me again." She smiled at Bonnie. "Come on, who was that boy just now?"

"Just someone I bumped into when a gang of yobs came charging through. I think he must be one of the Hungarians, and he's very ...um, very polite." Bonnie glanced over at the people waiting to pay their half-crowns to ride the scenic railway. "I don't fancy queuing, do you? We could try the Spanish Waltzer then move on to the Wall of Death if you like."

Kay was giving her a funny look. "If the boy you bumped into is a refugee, he's probably working on one of the rides. Oh, silly me! Could it be he has a job on the Spanish Waltzer?"

Bonnie was about to protest but both girls collapsed into giggles as they linked arms again.

"Patrik has beautiful brown eyes and a lovely voice."

"And suddenly you have a crush on him?" Kay glanced at her friend. "He must've gone through some very nasty experiences, if he was caught up in the Revolution. I'd steer clear if I were you. I bet your mum wouldn't approve of you seeing one of those refugees."

Bonnie felt indignant on Patrik's behalf. "You've no right to say that. And it's not fair to judge them all the same. I can't see any harm in taking a ride and saying hello again. I'm not running after him, if that's what you're thinking."

She stopped in her tracks as Kay muttered something Bonnie thought sounded like 'Take care he doesn't take **you** for a ride!'

"Anyway, what's so wonderful about Jack

Williams?" Bonnie argued. "You obviously didn't fall for him when you were sixteen. And just think of all that grease he works with now he's a mechanic. You can smell the Wall of Death long before you can see it."

"That's the fumes from the fuel, you daft aperth!"

They walked on in silence, Bonnie with her nose in the air. Past the shooting gallery with its rows of furry teddy bears and chubby-cheeked baby dolls waiting to be won and cuddled. Past the hoopla stall.

"Want to try your luck, girls?" the stallholder called to them, holding up a handful of multi-coloured rings. The hurdy-gurdy music boomed louder in Bonnie's ears now, as she shook her head.

"What's an aperth?" she asked Kay, unable to hold back her giggles. She and her best friend never fell out for long. "It's not a Welsh word, is it?"

"I've no idea," Kay said. She grinned. "I think Mum must have picked up some of my grampy's Yorkshire expressions. I'm sorry I was rude about the Hungarians." She linked arms with her friend once more.

"And I'm sorry for what I said about Jack."

"What was that boy called again?"

"Patrik. It's a lovely name, isn't it?"

"Isn't Patrick an Irish name?"

"Of course, but maybe it's spelt differently in Hungarian."

"Let's take a proper look at him, then. One ride on the Waltzer then off to watch motor bikes whizzing around!"

As she and Kay approached, Bonnie noticed the ride was slowing down. She spotted Patrik's dark hair as he operated the controls from his position inside a wooden booth. Suddenly he raised his head and looked straight at her. Once more, his serious expression vanished as that gorgeous smile she admired earlier showed a fun-loving, friendly side she guessed he'd learnt to keep well-hidden. Something about this boy appealed to her, though she couldn't say for sure what it might be.

Kay's sharp elbow jabbing her side made her gasp. "Is that him?" Her friend whispered.

"Thanks for cracking my ribs! Yes, that's Patrik."

"He's coming over. Shall I leave you alone?"

"No!" Bonnie grabbed her hand. "He's not coming to us specially. He has to make sure everyone gets out of the cars safely, as well as check new riders are fastened in securely."

"Ha! Well, that's told me, hasn't it? OK, the Waltzer isn't one of my favourite rides, but I'll put up with it for your sake."

Bonnie laughed. "That's how I feel about watching noisy motor bikes."

There was something very comforting about having the same friend from kindergarten and on through the grammar school years, she thought. You shared so many of the same experiences and each of you knew exactly what the other one liked or didn't. Kay had been longing to leave school and begin earning her own money. Bonnie had been keen to join the sixth form and study English, French and History at Advanced Level while still helping her mother.

Luckily, her mum could manage on her guest house earnings plus a modest widow's pension and Bonnie's late father had been careful to save money whilst on his long sea voyages. Now, after gaining a first-class secretarial diploma, she was hoping to find a suitable job so she could help her mother financially, though not until after the guest house's busy season ended.

The girls settled into their teacup shaped car and Bonnie's heartbeat bumped up a notch as Patrik stopped beside them and checked the grab rail was securely fastened. This was no ride for those who suffered from travel sickness. The cars rose and fell while the ride's circular base revolved, but also whisked around as well, disorientating the hapless riders. It was good fun, if you had a strong stomach and liked that sort of torture.

"Hello again," Patrik said, his attention fully on Bonnie.

"Hiya! This is my friend. Kay, meet Patrik."

Kay greeted him and the handsome Hungarian nodded and held out his hand to her before checking the girls were safely fastened in. "I have to shoot everybody off now. I see you later."

To her credit, Kay hadn't burst out laughing or teased Patrik about using the wrong word. "I think he meant start everybody off now," Bonnie said once he moved away.

"I do hope so!" Kay nudged her. "He is rather lush though. Gorgeous eyes. I don't blame you for falling for him."

"Who said anything about falling for him?"

But Bonnie forgot everything except holding tight to the safety rail as the cars, which had set off so gently, began twirling and whirling around while the riders were lifted up and down. Her right leg was glued to Kay's left leg as they tried to keep their bottoms on the seat. Over the loudspeaker, Pat Boone was singing the praises of *Bernadine* while the teacup car lurched and swayed and rocked and rolled.

"This is crazy!" Kay said after a while. "Why on earth did we wear these frilly petticoats? I can't hold my skirt down as well as cling to the rail!"

Bonnie couldn't answer for laughing. Sometimes the ride operators switched on machines to blow air at the riders. The current fashion for circular skirts and layers of net petticoats made the girls prime targets for this trick. But at last, they were slowing down...

"Phew," Kay said. "I'd forgotten what an endurance test this ride is."

"It's a good job we didn't have an ice cream before we went on!"

They awaited their turn to be set free while Patrik, joined by another young man, released the dishevelled riders. Bonnie felt as though she'd taken a turbulent trip in a speedboat, but as Patrik took her hand to help her out, she enjoyed a little thrill of anticipation running down her spine. He squeezed her fingers before letting her go, then gallantly assisted Kay out too.

"I see you again soon? Please, Bonnie?"

Her heart would soon be a puddle. Who could resist those puppy dog eyes? But apart from being unsure how to respond, she reminded herself how she'd been let down so badly by her last boyfriend. And, what about Kay's warning to beware of someone in such a vulnerable situation? Her friend could be scatty, but she did have a point.

As Kay wandered towards the Wall of Death, Bonnie held her breath. She didn't quite know what to say next.

"I don't have money to spare. So sorry. Would you come for a walk with me some time?" He swallowed hard. "I like to talk to you, Bonnie. Learn about you. Is possible?"

"I'm so sorry, Patrik. I have a lot on my plate at the moment."

He frowned. "Your plate is too full?"

Bonnie tried not to look as if her heart was dancing a jig. "Sorry – I mean I have lots to do." She bit her lip. "I help my mother run her guest house and Saturdays are turnover days."

"What is this turnover? You make pastry on

Saturdays?"

She chuckled. "Sorry, Patrik. I'm not laughing at you. I think your English is very good. Turnover days are when one lot of guests move out and new ones move in. My mother needs Kay and me to help strip the beds and make up the rooms again. There's washing to do and everything..." Helplessly, she gazed up at him. He must realise this was peak season. After all, he wouldn't have a job at the pleasure park but for that.

"Of course. I understand. When good for you then? I have Monday off but in the morning that day, I wash cars for a taxi firm."

"Goodness, we're both so busy, aren't we?" She thought for a moment. No, it was best not to get involved. Didn't she want to start a night school course in September? There were books to be read before then. Besides, she and this young man came from two different countries. Two very different worlds. She took a deep breath. "I'm sure we'll meet again, Patrik. I'll see you around."

He nodded; his face still solemn. "I understand." He took her hand and kissed it.

Bonnie sucked in her breath as she felt the soft touch of his lips against her skin. Above them, the sky was a sea of sugared-almond colours, a palette of pale blues, pinks and mauves. All around them, lights were going on, twinkling like fireflies. The rides would remain open until ten o'clock. Friday nights were on a par with Saturdays for trade.

"I have to find Kay now," she said. "Goodbye, Patrik."

She heard him say, 'See you around,' as she turned away.

She counted slowly to ten before looking back to watch him take his place in the booth. But as she drew closer to the Wall of Death, where stunt motorcyclists thrilled audiences with their amazing feats, she realised something was wrong. What was that shouting? Frantic cries for help sent Bonnie hurrying to the big wooden drum. She scampered up the nearest flight of steps, but the onlookers peering down from the viewing platform were mostly still and silent now. Almost as though they were afraid to move. And there was no sign of Kay.

Bonnie wriggled into a space and looked over the barricade, sandwiched between two people. Fierce flames and a plume of black smoke were rising from below. Someone must have switched off the music. Was it her imagination, or were those fiery tongues leaping higher and higher? Would this blaze suddenly become an inferno?

CHAPTER 2

Bonnie scanned the faces around the circle but still couldn't see her friend. Her mouth dried as she clattered down the wooden steps again. Began running around the stand. Calling Kay's name. Trying to understand what was going on. A sudden bang caused several girls to start screaming again. One or two onlookers began scrambling down the flights of steps connecting the viewing platform with the ground. Somewhere, a child was crying. And the acrid smell of burning oil was causing people to cough and splutter.

"Help! Someone dial 999! Quick!" Someone yelled from above.

Bonnie wondered where the nearest telephone box was. She couldn't remember. Did any of these ride operators have a phone in their kiosks? She had no idea. And the fire seemed to be roaring louder. An angry beast. Heat rising from the base of the drum …

"Move! All peoples on top come downstairs at once. Please go careful on the steps. Ladies and children first!"

She recognised that voice. But what was Patrik doing here when he worked on another ride? She stood watching as she saw the onlookers reacting exactly as he'd instructed. A man shouted he was going to phone 999. She watched him run off, noticing he had the presence of mind to barge into the nearest café where they were sure to have a telephone. Patrik's arrival seemed to have jolted people out of their shocked state.

"Thank God, someone's using a fire extinguisher!" Another man shouted the news on his way down to the ground.

Bonnie noticed his gaudy Hawaiian shirt, its pattern of exotic birds and palm trees so vivid against the drab wooden cylinder. What if the breeze should send sparks flying towards the dry wood? Bonnie groaned. It didn't bear thinking about.

Then Kay was racing towards her, dark-chestnut ponytail bobbing as she ran. The girls clung on to one another, Kay coughing, then babbling about Jack and how he'd been about to come out and speak to her when she heard some kind of explosion and people began screaming and suddenly Jack was no longer there.

"Hey, I'm sure he'll be OK," Bonnie soothed her friend. "I saw him inside the dome when I climbed the steps, looking for you." She nudged Kay. "Look, there he is with that fire extinguisher. With any luck, they'll get the flames under control, but I doubt they'll give any more performances this evening." She couldn't help looking round for Patrik, then realised he must have returned to his own job.

"Do you mind if we hang around to make sure Jack's OK?"

"No, of course I don't mind."

Kay sniffed loudly. "That awful smell! It was difficult to breathe over there."

Bonnie frowned. "Burning oil's bound to smell disgusting. Are you sure you're alright? We should probably get away and breathe in some sea air."

Kay shook her head. "I must see Jack before we go. It's difficult to explain ...I'll tell you later."

Bonnie nodded. She looked around and saw most of

the onlookers were drifting off, now it seemed there were no casualties.

"Jack! Oh, thank goodness you're all right." Now Kay was hurrying towards Jack Williams who'd spotted her and begun walking towards her. His face was covered in dark smudges but he was smiling.

To Bonnie's surprise, her friend stopped in her tracks and stood motionless, as though uncertain what to do next. She wasn't usually what you'd call shy. Of the two girls, Kay was usually the more outspoken and far more at ease with the opposite sex. She'd had two years since school earning her own money, while Bonnie's existence was much more sheltered. Yet here she was, reacting exactly as Jack was – as if they wanted to rush into one another's arms, like the American lieutenant and the English nurse, the hero and heroine of Bonnie's mum's favourite book, *Farewell to Arms*. Bonnie wondered if, for once in her life, Kay was shy about showing her true feelings.

"Bonnie!"

She spun round at the sound of her name. "Goodness, Patrik, that fire could have been disastrous, couldn't it?"

The Hungarian looked uncertain.

"I mean, lots of people might've needed first aid if it hadn't been for some of the men's quick reactions." She walked towards him. "That's including you, of course. I saw you trying to get spectators to come down to ground level."

He shrugged. "I am sorry to say I have been close to many fires and shootings in my country. I think my – my way of reaction is tuned in. Your friend is good, yes?" He nodded towards Kay and Jack while Bonnie watched him smile in that tummy-lurching way again. What was happening to her, for goodness' sake?

She wondered where Patrik had found board and lodgings. Surely, he couldn't be sleeping on the pleasure park? Her mouth felt dry. She needed to drink something. Before she could move, a voice boomed over the public address system while she and the young Hungarian stood listening.

"They close the park early tonight," Patrik said. He nodded towards Kay and Jack. "Kay is going with her boyfriend, yes?"

Bonnie glanced at the pair and saw they were holding hands while they talked. "I don't know. They haven't been boyfriend and girlfriend for ages. Meeting again this evening was sheer chance."

It was hard to read Patrik's expression in the half-twilight, half electronic glare of their surroundings, but she knew he was puzzled.

"It's complicated," she said. "I'll find out what's going on."

"My boss is locking up now," Patrik said. "I can walk you home if your friend Kay doesn't want to go with you."

Bonnie hesitated. "But you don't know where I live."

"Is no problem. I am used to walking long ways."

He was so matter-of-fact. So resigned. Her heart went out to him.

"I'll be back in a minute." Bonnie hurried across the concourse to speak to her friend, returning moments later.

"They want to go to the café. If I know anything about Kay, she'll be after a lift home on the back of Jack's moped. Are you thirsty?"

He held his head high. "I have not money to buy peoples a drink. Is best I wait for you outside, then happy to see you home safe and sound."

"Please, won't you come with us? Kay and I've

agreed we'll treat you and Jack to a cold drink as a little thank you for what you did tonight."

"Is no need." He still held his head high.

"I think there is. Please say you'll join us. Then, yes, I'd appreciate you seeing me home. It's not far to walk, although the last part sometimes makes people puff and pant a bit!"

What was she doing? She wasn't afraid of walking home on her own. But some extra time with this young man was too hard to resist.

Bonnie thought Jack seemed surprised to find the Hungarian boy joining them. He didn't say much at first and appeared a little withdrawn, but everyone understood Jack had gone through something unpleasant and frightening and Kay in particular could chatter enough for the four of them. The atmosphere improved when both young men realised they shared a love of football. After they finished their ice-cream sodas and Bonnie had been teased about the long glass it was served in being almost as tall as she was, they left the café together.

By this time, Kay and Jack were hand in hand again. Kay was obviously agonising as to whether it was fair to abandon Bonnie to walking home on her own, but Patrik insisted he would see his new friend back to her house safely and Jack chimed in, saying he knew Patrik was respected by the fun fair people and known to be very reliable.

Bonnie's cheeks needed fanning when she heard this, fearing the young Hungarian would suspect she'd been quizzing Jack to make sure she'd be safe in Patrik's company. But after saying their goodnights to Kay and Jack, Patrik seemed much more relaxed, although to Bonnie's relief, he made no attempt to hold hands or put his arm around her waist. The sensible part of her knew it was best not to let her tumbling emotions overwhelm her. She and Kay and the boys had all gone through a few turbulent hours and not only because of the Spanish Waltzer or the Wall of Death.

"How many peoples can stay in your guest house at one time?" Patrik asked as he and Bonnie strolled along the promenade, now much quieter than it had been earlier. A few folk still sat on the benches, gazing at the setting sun; a molten orange globe fast sinking into the inky waters of the Bristol Channel.

"We have six letting rooms," Bonnie said with more than a touch of pride. "But my mother has a couple of cots and in four of the rooms there's a single bed as well, so two young children can easily share that. One of the rooms is kept specially for honeymooners." At once she felt self-conscious and hoped Patrik understood that expression so she didn't have to explain it.

No such luck! "What is this word, honeymooners, please?"

They were climbing the hill leading to home now. Ahead of them, a couple were strolling, arms around one another's waists. The man was no taller than the young woman and Bonnie recognised these two as guests at *Sea Breezes*. They were in Room Number 1, the bedroom known as the honeymoon suite. The husband liked baked beans with his egg, bacon and sausage and his wife preferred half a grilled tomato. Her mother said, even if they hadn't booked the superior accommodation, they were clearly honeymooners, though Bonnie hadn't yet developed the knack of identifying newly-weds.

She swallowed hard. "Honeymooners is a word we use to describe two people who are spending a holiday together, having just become man and wife. Well, usually it's newly-married couples who go on honeymoon, though I suppose some people have to delay going until they've saved up enough money or got enough leave from work."

"So, I learn another new word. Do many honeymooners come here? I think it is probably special place to spend a holiday."

"I think we've had our fair share of them over the years," she said, inwardly praying Patrik wouldn't ask for further details. Her mother had several funny as well as embarrassing stories up her sleeve, but no way did Bonnie intend revealing them. She cast round for a safe subject to talk about, but didn't dare ask him about life in his home country. In his turn, he must have many desperately sad and unforgettable experiences tucked away in his memory. She was about to ask how he was liking British food when he spoke again. And the subject could not have been further away from moonlight, or roses or baked beans.

"I have been studying before I leave Hungary," he said. "I not want you to think I have no good brain."

She felt humbled. "I would never think any such thing, Patrik. The way you're succeeding in speaking English tells me you must be clever. I'd be hopeless if I was suddenly made to speak a foreign language. Unless it was French," she said. "I enjoy speaking French."

"Then you must be clever girl," he said, turning his head to smile at her. "So, when you finish making beds and serving breakfasts, you go back to college or you ready to take up career?"

"I need to begin job hunting soon. I have my secretarial diploma, but I doubt I'll find anything that requires me to use my knowledge of French. Mum says maybe I should apply for teacher training, but I'm fed up with exams." She hesitated. "Am I speaking too quickly for you?"

"Not too fast. I keep up, just about!"

Each of them laughed at the same time and Bonnie hoped he didn't think she was talking down to him. He really had a very good command of English, but she couldn't guess how long he'd been in Great Britain.

"You not want to be a teacher because you say you are soon ready to look for job in an office?"

"I'd like to earn my own money as soon as possible. And I find the thought of three more years of studying a little daunting, to be honest."

"Ah. I am stuck with daunting word."

"Off-putting? We use the word 'intimidating' but that has five syllables." She thought for a moment. "If we're talking about facing something we have to do, we might find whatever it was, daunting."

"Bravo! I now have perfect understanding of the word which is daunting. Thank you, Bonnie. You make good teacher."

"You're a quick learner. Tell me what you were studying in Hungary before you, I mean when ..."

"I was studying ophthalmology, Bonnie. Five syllables word, yes?"

She laughed. "But how amazing! I mean, what a brilliant thing to do. How were you getting on?"

He didn't answer for a few moments. Maybe he was afraid of disclosing too much. After all, they'd only met one another that evening. You couldn't blame him for not wanting to give away his personal history.

They'd reached the top of the hill. She could see the golden glow of the guest house porch light just along the row of former merchant navy captains' residences. The honeymooners must have already gone indoors.

Then, all of a sudden, a tall man was striding towards them. To Bonnie's surprise, he was calling her name.

CHAPTER 3

"Mr Hamilton? What's up? Is my mother all right?" Bonnie ran forward, afraid to imagine just what Charlie Hamilton, a frequent visitor to *Sea Breezes,* could possibly want with her.

"Your mother was worried about you, Bonnie, so I said I'd walk down to the prom and see if I could find you. The couple who just came back told us about the fire at the Wall of Death." Charlie's gaze moved to Bonnie's escort, who was now standing protectively beside her.

"Oh, my goodness, poor Mum! I'm fine. We're all fine. This is Patrik, but I'd best get straight inside and prove to my mother I'm still in one piece." She turned to her new friend. "Thank you so much for walking me home."

"Is my pleasure."

Charlie Hamilton cleared his throat. "As long as you're all right. Could you tell your mother I'm taking a stroll down to the prom, now we know you're safe and sound? I've done a lot of driving today and need to stretch my legs. 'Night, Bonnie." He nodded to Patrik and set off; his pace much more leisurely now.

Patrik made a polite little bow to Bonnie, his gesture promptly turning her insides to squishy marshmallow. He was such a courteous young man. Courteous and far too handsome.

"Goodnight, Bonnie. You know where to find me."

"Of course. Thanks for walking me back and I'll see you soon. That's a promise Patrik."

Upon impulse, she stood on tiptoe and planted a light kiss on his left cheek. Then she hurried up the six wide stone steps leading to the guest house front door and let herself inside.

The young Hungarian remained standing, motionless in the pool of light beneath the street lamp. At last, he raised his left hand and touched his cheek where Bonnie had kissed him. He gave the front door of *Sea Breezes* one last lingering look before setting off the way he'd come.

As he turned the corner and took the slope down to the promenade, he was startled by a dark figure he saw crossing the road towards him. At once he tensed, balling his fists, ready to defend himself from a mugger if necessary. Pure instinct caused him to call out "What do you want?" in his own language.

"Hey, I didn't mean to give you a shock, Patrik. It is Patrik, isn't it?" The tall man who'd been looking for Bonnie came up to him, holding out his hand. "Miss Morgan didn't have time to introduce us properly. My name's Charlie Hamilton and I'm a sales representative. I've known Diane Morgan and her daughter for several years now. Forgive me if I appear over-protective, but I'd like to talk to you. I hope you don't mind if I keep you company on the way down to the promenade?"

The two men began walking down the hill together. Patrik, completely at a loss as to what this man could possibly want with him, kept silent. He was skilled at clamming up when the occasion demanded. The Englishman, he thought, must be of good character, if what he said about knowing Bonnie and her mother well was true. But Hamilton had obviously hung around on the opposite pavement, waiting for him to appear. What could this mean? Was he some kind of official?

Patrik felt his stomach lurch as dread crept through him, though he couldn't think of anything he might have done wrong. The cool evening breeze made him aware of perspiration on his brow and he raised one hand to wipe away the dampness.

His companion gave him a swift sideways glance. "I mean you no harm, Patrik. Is it all right for me to call you by your first name?"

"Is fine, yes."

"And how about you call me Charlie? I expect you're wondering why I didn't head straight down to the prom, ay, Patrik?"

Patrik noticed Charlie Hamilton had a slight lisp. This meant he pronounced Patrik's name as 'Patwik' but said it so quickly, it was hardly noticeable.

"Now, I don't intend delaying you this evening because I know you need to grab as much sleep as you can get. Am I right?"

"You are right, sir – I mean, Charlie."

"Since last autumn, you and many more of your countrymen have been forced to flee Hungary and make a new life for yourselves in other parts of Europe. How long have you been in South Wales, Patrik?"

The Hungarian hesitated.

"Just for the record, I don't hold any position of authority."

"I do not really understand," Patrik said.

"Sorry, son. I mean I'm not any kind of policeman or immigration officer. I make my living by working as a sales representative, which means I sell all kinds of things to gift shops and places such as roller-skating rinks and social clubs. Golden Sands is on my patch and while it's high season with the holidaymakers here in their droves, I'm spending extra time in this town. Makes good business sense."

"I see." For the life of him, Patrik couldn't understand what all this had to do with him. But he was relieved the older man posed no threat.

"Are you alone or did anyone else travel with you? I ask only out of friendly curiosity."

"My elder brother is here for three months already. He is master plumber back home and he has found work in the town. I came with two friends to join him but Luca no longer with us." His voice faltered. "I try to forget some things, you know?"

"I can imagine. I'm so sorry."

"And my other friend, he goes to London to find work. He likes to train to become chef."

"You don't look more than twenty to me, Patrik. What did you do for a job back in Hungary?"

"I am almost twenty-one and I was learning to become ophthalmologist." Patrik pronounced the separate syllables slowly. "Another year of the course to go but no good to me now. I feel passionate about helping peoples to keep their eyesight, but who knows how I can go about it, now I am in foreign country?"

Charlie whistled. "But you've done extremely well. I'm very impressed." He was silent as they began walking along the promenade. "In fact, so impressed that I'd like to help you realise your dream. Might I ask what job they've given you at the pleasure park?"

"How you know where I work?" Patrik still wasn't entirely at ease.

"It's not difficult to guess, son. I imagine you and Miss Morgan met earlier this evening, got talking and took a shine – I mean took a liking to one another and you, being the gentleman that you are, offered to walk her home. Am I right?"

"You are right. Is some problem?"

"No, not at all. I'm glad you found yourself a job while you're sorting things out. I hope you're not having to sleep rough though?"

The young Hungarian hesitated. "How rough?"

"I mean camping in the open air, or kipping down on someone's floor, that kind of thing."

"I have bunk with three others in caravan owned by boss. Is OK."

"Well, that's something anyway. Tell you what, Patrik, why don't we meet tomorrow or Sunday, whichever's best for you? I'll treat you to a nice meal. Just tell me what time you're free for an hour, there's a good lad. I have something in mind that might be to your advantage."

Bonnie poked her head round the door of the residents' lounge where two couples were chatting over cups of tea, and asked them how their day had gone. When she went through to the little room adjoining the lounge, she found her mother sitting at the roll top desk, working. She turned her head as her daughter hurried over to give her a hug.

"Bonnie! What's been going on?"

"Mum, I'm sorry to hear you've been worrying about us. Luckily nobody was injured. A mechanic working on the Wall of Death told us one of the motor bikes had a fuel leak and a spark set off a small fire which might have got much worse. Luckily nobody was injured."

"Oh dear, were you anywhere near, love?"

"Not really. Kay was though. She used to go out with Jack, the mechanic, so she, um, she'd gone over to find him just as the fire started. But she wasn't in any danger."

"Good, but I hope that doesn't mean you had to hang around on your own too long?" Diane Morgan folded the last resident's bill ready for the morning and sat back in the chair, looking expectantly at her daughter.

"No, we went to a café for an ice cream soda and I honestly didn't think you might hear about the fire until I was almost here and met Mr Hamilton."

"Well, luckily I didn't have to wait long before you got back, love." Her mother smiled at her. "Everyone's safely in now, except for Charlie."

"Oh, I should have said! He asked me to tell you he fancied stretching his legs so he was going to walk down to the prom."

Bonnie's mother raised her eyebrows. "You seem a bit flummoxed, love, but. I expect it's understandable, given what happened tonight. Why don't I make you a nice cup of Bournvita?"

"Thanks, but I don't fancy a milky drink. Is there anything you want me to do before I go on up?"

"No, you go ahead. I'll collect the tea things when those two couples turn in. You get a good night's sleep and I'll wait up for Mr Hamilton. He doesn't usually keep me hanging about long, but I've got my library book to keep me company. I'm halfway through *Death on the Nile* now."

"OK. I don't know how you manage to keep your eyes open!" She kissed her mother's cheek. "Night-Night."

On her way up to bed, Bonnie wondered how easy it would be for her to get to sleep. The evening had sizzled with unexpected events. But fortunately, she'd managed not to let her mum know who walked her home and how they came to meet. She needed to examine her feelings before going near the pleasure park again. Because the look of tenderness in Patrik's eyes when they'd had a quiet moment while standing near the Waltzer and later as he looked at her across the café table, sent a wave of something sweet yet disturbing, rippling through her body.

She closed her bedroom door behind her and thought of her former sweetheart and how she'd considered him to be a good friend until he dropped her without warning. Even after the brief time spent with Patrik that evening, she recognised how different she already felt. Could this strange, new emotion really be love?

CHAPTER 4

The moment she awoke next morning to find sunshine streaming through her daisy-patterned curtains, Bonnie thought of the young Hungarian. She checked the time on her alarm clock, grinned and stretched her arms high above her head before snuggling down again. Five more precious minutes in her own private world! But although daydreaming was fun, she knew it would be a mistake to go to the Spanish Waltzer after finishing work. She daren't risk getting Patrik into trouble with his boss, by hanging around the ride.

Anyway, Saturdays, being changeover day, involved extra work. Every bed having been occupied this week required a set of fresh linen. Her mother, Kay and herself would have their work cut out to clear away the breakfast things before making a start on the housekeeping chores. New arrivals would be turning up any time from three o'clock onwards.

She wondered where Patrik stayed. Might he live with others in the same situation? And was he awake at this moment too? Thinking about her, even? Heat flooded Bonnie's cheeks as she imagined him lying in bed, maybe even wondering whether she'd been telling the truth when she promised to see him soon. Now, with the start of a new day and a clear head, she knew full well how much she wanted this to happen.

But many of the townsfolk were wary of the new arrivals. Her mother had already informed her of that, well before Bonnie's encounter with Patrik. Bonnie decided she mustn't tell Diane what was going on. But was anything actually going on? Last night, she'd met a boy she liked and he seemed to have liked her back. But perhaps she wasn't the first girl to catch the Hungarian's eye?

Bonnie reached across to stop her alarm from shrilling. She'd nip into the bathroom before her mother got up, and start the day on the right foot. Kay would arrive, no doubt eager to chatter about Jack and how much he'd changed and probably how he'd asked her for a date, even though he must work almost every evening. The Wall of Death needed its mechanics on hand to deal with any break downs or other problems. Yesterday's mishap had proved that.

But if her friend was eager to know how Bonnie had got on with Patrik, it would be better not to give away any secrets. Far wiser to act as though he was nice enough, but not someone Bonnie would seriously consider as a boyfriend. She had no intention of sounding snobbish or critical about him or any of his friends, come to that. But she needed to keep her head and not rush into a situation she might later regret. And when Kay arrived for work, Bonnie decided to warn her not to mention Patrik to Bonnie's mother. The snag was, would Charlie Hamilton tease her when he came down to breakfast?

Bonnie hurried downstairs, neatly dressed in navy cotton dirndl skirt with her sleeveless white blouse tucked into the skirt's waistband. She'd beaten her mum to it so filled the big kettle ready to brew a pot of tea for the workers, plus one for those guests who liked tea in bed before starting their day. Once all the guests had tucked into their cooked breakfasts, with everything cleared away, she and Kay usually had something to eat while Mrs Morgan preferred to wait until later, when she could steal twenty minutes or so in private.

Bonnie took four cups of tea upstairs to the first floor and returned to the kitchen when, surprisingly, Kay tapped at the back door before Bonnie's mum made an appearance. Bonnie pulled the door bolt back and Kay erupted into the kitchen, her eyes shining. She immediately began babbling about what Jack had said and the plans he had for his future.

"And good morning to you too, Kay Smith!" Bonnie shook her head. "What time did you get indoors last night? Sounds as if Jack really poured his heart out to you." She chuckled. "Let's pour you a cuppa, shall we?"

"Thanks, Bonnie. We were chatting by the front gate for ages, until my dad tapped on the window and I had to go inside. Jack wants me to meet him this afternoon when he has his tea break." Kay looked around. "Where's your mum? I hope she's not poorly."

"Not as far as I know, but I think I'll take her a cup of tea in a minute being as she may have been kept up late last night. Mr Hamilton still hadn't got back when I climbed the wooden hill." Bonnie decided not to tell her friend he'd come looking for her then continued down to the promenade. Patrik couldn't have been far behind him.

But Bonnie's mother walked in moments later, calling a cheerful 'Good morning girls' as usual.

Bonnie noticed suspicious dark smudges beneath her eyes. "I hope you weren't kept up too late, Mum?"

Diane Morgan groaned. "Charlie came back in talkative mood and we sat putting the world to rights until gone midnight. I didn't like to seem unsociable but

I could have done without a late night before our busy Saturday." She sipped her tea, gratefully. "And I might be going out this evening, for a change."

Bonnie had other things on her mind. "So, we're not likely to see Charlie down for breakfast much before nine?"

"I've no idea, love. Do you have something planned for later?"

Bonnie ignored Kay's raised eyebrows. "Nothing special, but I thought I'd walk up to the library this afternoon so I can change my books. Is that OK with you?"

"It's fine, love." Her mum glanced at the kitchen clock. "Time to get the bacon started." She consulted her list. "Kay, you might as well take the honeymooners their tea now. They said they were in no hurry to set off back."

"Course I will. I'll bang on the door loudly and make sure they know I'm there before I take in the tray."

Bonnie daren't look at her mother. Kay could be a little outspoken sometimes. But it seemed Diane was concentrating upon separating bacon rashers before getting them sizzling beneath the gas grill.

"Bonnie, about this evening – I know it's short notice, but would you mind staying in? Unless you've already made plans ...?"

Bonnie felt a mixture of relief and disappointment. If Kay wanted an escort when she went to see Jack at the pleasure park, she'd have to make do without her best friend. "If you want to go out, Mum, I'll make sure I'm here. Going somewhere special?"

Her mother coloured up. "Charlie has two tickets for a dinner dance in Cardiff. One of those retail trade things, he said. Sprang it on me last night and it seemed like a good idea at the time. What do you think?"

"What do I think? You definitely deserve a night out. You hardly ever go anywhere and you could wear your turquoise cocktail dress. You haven't worn it since you went to that Christmas dance at the town hall." Bonnie walked over to the cooker and whispered in her mum's ear, "I've always suspected Mr Hamilton of having a soft spot for you."

"Nonsense! He's a divorced man and I'm a few years older than he is so there's no chance of me getting serious about him, lovey. It's just that being able to put on a pretty frock for once and eat a dinner I haven't cooked sounds too good to miss." She plonked a loaf of bread on the cutting board and began slicing it for toast.

Bonnie knew her mother still sorely missed her late husband. But she had resisted any overtures from older local widowers and Bonnie wasn't surprised to hear her opinion of Charlie Hamilton. One night out with someone she'd known for several years, with no strings attached, sounded harmless enough, surely? Bonnie started cutting thick slices of tomato ready to fry. A big pan of baked beans stood nearby. The breakfast drill never varied and Bonnie sometimes thought she could complete it in her sleep.

She was wondering whether her new Hungarian friend would expect her to visit the fun fair that evening, or not. But she hardly had time to speculate because Kay was back, not only still carrying the tea tray, but wearing a puzzled expression upon her face.

"What's up?" Bonnie put down her knife.

"I'm not sure. I can't find the honeymooners!"

Bonnie's mum turned around to face Kay. "Say that again?"

"Mr and Mrs White aren't in their room, Mrs Morgan. I wondered if they'd gone straight into the dining room so I came back down, but there's no sign of them there."

Diane gasped. "Don't tell me their luggage has gone?"

Kay looked anguished. "I didn't think to check! Shall I go back?"

"Leave it to me. I'll soon find out if they've done a runner." With that, she left the room and the girls exchanged glances as they heard her hurrying upstairs.

"How awful if they've left without paying their bill." Bonnie's heart beat faster than usual as she contemplated this possibility.

"Gosh, shall I see if the front door's unlocked? If they did leave in the night, they couldn't have bolted the door behind them."

"That's true. Yes, please check so you can tell Mum. I need to turn this bacon over."

But Diane Morgan was back, just as Kay returned, a concerned expression upon her face. "The front door's been left unbolted," she said.

"What's going on? Is everything all right, ladies?" Charlie Hamilton appeared in the doorway.

"It seems I've been swindled, Charlie, that's what's going on. The honeymoon couple who've been with us since last Saturday have done a moonlight flit. They must have crept down in the small hours and let themselves out." She shook her head. "They arrived by car – otherwise, they could never have left when there are no trains and taxis in the middle of the night."

"Mum, why don't I go upstairs and check they haven't left any money in the room? I can't believe they'd vanish without paying their bill."

"Sensible girl, Bonnie," Charlie chipped in. "It's unlikely, in my opinion, but you need to check. Look on the bright side!"

"They asked for their bill last night," Diane said. "I

handed it to the husband when they came back and he said he'd write a cheque."

"There you are, then. What's the betting Bonnie will come back with a cheque in her hand?"

"But, Charlie, why would they leave like thieves in the night? It doesn't make sense."

"A lovers' tiff? Decided they'd had enough of all the lovebird stuff and couldn't wait to get back to normal?" Charlie shrugged. "I'm just guessing, but there has to be some rational explanation."

"Goodness, I sincerely hope so!"

He looked over his shoulder. "There's a couple coming downstairs now. The husband reminds me of that Jimmy Edwards."

Kay was looking blank as she heated some lard ready for frying eggs.

"You know, the comedian with the handlebar moustache?" Charlie said. "I'll go and pass the time of day with them, but I won't mention anything about the honeymooners. If I were you, I wouldn't say a word to any of the guests about this, Diane."

He headed for the dining room as Bonnie came into the kitchen. "There's no sign of any envelope or cheque, or pound notes left anywhere in the room. I even looked inside the Bible in the bedside drawer."

"Thank you, Bonnie. Then I need to report this to the Police. I've no idea how long it'll take, but I know you two will cope OK."

Charlie Hamilton volunteered to take breakfast orders so the girls could deal with the food without interruption. Kay saw to the teas, coffees and toast while Bonnie dished up the savoury treats which guests had been complimenting her mother on throughout the week. At last, all five couples were happily eating and chatting.

Charlie insisted he'd skip breakfast that morning as he didn't want to risk being late for his early appointment and needed to leave the guest-house well before nine o'clock. He took a cup of tea into the residents' lounge.

By the time Bonnie's mum put her head round the door of the kitchen, some guests had paid Bonnie for their stay and left.

"They're sending two policemen round," Diane said. "I'd better let Mr Hamilton know, just in case he decides to wait and see them."

But when she gave Charlie the news, he hurriedly drank the rest of his tea and got to his feet. "Thanks, Diane, but I'm afraid I need to get moving. I hope you've remembered our dinner date this evening. You mustn't let yourself get too upset by that couple's behaviour. I know it's disappointing for you, but in this business, I'm afraid it's bound to happen now and then."

"It's just that those two were so friendly – so appreciative of everything we did for them. It's hard to believe they could behave so badly. I keep hoping they'll ring up, all in a flap because they decided to leave so early, they forgot about paying their bill."

Charlie patted her on the shoulder. "You always think the best of people, Diane, but it's unlikely, I'm afraid. If, as I suspect, they're con artists, they'll be skilful at playing every guest-house owner's ideal guests. And, being a honeymoon couple – which I have my doubts about anyway – they have every excuse not to mingle with other guests and risk getting into a conversation that might later incriminate them."

Bonnie overheard this comment as she came in to clear tables. "Goodness, do you really suspect that couple of making a habit of defrauding people, Mr Hamilton?"

"I'm afraid so. But the police will have their own

ideas. Best you leave the honeymooners' bedroom untouched until the cops arrive. And I think they'll want to interview all of you, in order to learn as much as possible about that young man and woman."

"Oh dear." Diane bit her lip. "The policeman I spoke to didn't say anything about asking the departing guests to remain on the premises. Several have already left, so I hope I shan't get ticked off."

"All of them had trains to catch," Bonnie said. "I shouldn't worry, Mum. Anyway, it's too late now."

Charlie Hamilton excused himself, saying he needed to return to his room, but would be leaving immediately afterwards.

Once he'd gone upstairs, Bonnie looked at her mother. "Mr Hamilton doesn't usually have an early appointment on a Saturday, does he?"

Diane stared back at her. "I hadn't thought about it. But as it's high season, he's probably trying to fit more calls in. It's good that he has more customers to visit, isn't it? Good for him and extra income for us."

Bonnie nodded and headed to the kitchen, carrying a laden tray of used cutlery and crockery. On her next trip to the dining-room she noticed her mother saying goodbye to Charlie, and both of them were unaware of Bonnie's presence at the other end of the hallway.

"Hope all goes well," Charlie said, kissing her mother on the cheek. "Um... be a darling and don't volunteer me as a witness, Diane. I can't give any information that could possibly assist the cops in their investigation. OK?"

"Of course. I'm sure there's no need for you to be troubled, Charlie. You're a busy man."

"I do have a lot of calls to make today, so I really need to be on my way now."

"I hope it all goes well for you. I'll see you later on."

"We should leave here at six-thirty on the dot."

"I'll make sure I'm ready." Diane gave him a big smile.

As she went about her tasks, Bonnie couldn't help wondering why Mr Hamilton seemed so anxious to leave the guesthouse before the police turned up. She'd once heard him say he didn't like arriving too early at shops and amusement arcades, preferring to let his customers ease their way into the day before he tried coaxing them into ordering some new line or other.

Bonnie told herself it was none of her business but something about the sales rep made her wonder whether her mother was doing the right thing by becoming closer to him. And how could she possibly criticise her own mum for seeking male companionship, when she herself was very aware that people who knew her would probably see lovely Patrik as a foreigner in their midst and possibly unsuitable as a boyfriend?

CHAPTER 5

Patrik Matyaz, at twenty-one years of age, had like many others born in 1936, experienced a lot more drama and hardship than those born a decade later, despite that decade's world war. Apart from his brother, he was distanced from the remaining members of their family and he lacked a father figure in his life. So, he was intrigued by Charlie Hamilton's interest in him and had agreed to meet for breakfast in a small café at the far end of the promenade.

Patrik arrived first and perched on the low stone wall separating the promenade from the stretch of grass and flower beds overlooking the sea. His back to the beach, he tried to guess what this meeting was all about. But it wasn't long before he wondered whether Bonnie might make an appearance later that day. If only he had the money to treat her to a meal out or a cinema or dance. He closed his eyes briefly, enjoying the feel of the morning sunshine, as he traced back a childhood memory.

He couldn't have been more than eight years of age but he clearly recalled an afternoon in the garden at his parents' home. His father had been a teacher and his mother planning to find work in a library as she'd been employed as a librarian before Patrik's elder sisters and brother began to arrive.

All four siblings had been in the garden as well as cousins. One of his uncles was playing the violin while Patrik's mother sang and the children jigged around, linking hands and laughing until Patrik got the hiccups! He remembered the music had been lively though couldn't put a name to it. There had been food and drink, homemade bread, cold meats and spicy sausages. Sponge cake – the layers sandwiched together with chocolate cream and chopped walnuts. If he closed his eyes, he could almost taste it.

But he opened his eyes immediately. His mother and father had gone. Like so many others, he mustn't look back. His parents would want him to make a life for himself in this strange new land called Great Britain. Here he felt safe. He slept well at night, unafraid of bangs upon the door, no longer dreading the sound of screams and shots. His brother, Istvan, worked hard, determined to own his own plumbing business one day. Patrik admired him for that, but somehow, somewhere, he must find a better job for himself.

Only then could he hope to apply for more training to qualify for the career he longed to follow. Already his English was improving. He smiled as he thought of Bonnie. She was kind and patient as well as pretty. She worked hard in her mother's boarding house and she too wanted to become better-qualified.

Patrik was under no illusion. He was aware some people were suspicious and resentful of the arrival of strangers from overseas. He had heard mutterings, though to be fair, not amongst the men and the handful of women working on the pleasure park. And especially not Jack, who always gave him a cheery greeting and had told Patrik how much his help was appreciated when the fire broke out at the Wall of Death. No, these people who worked hard so others might enjoy a few hours of fun away from their daily grind were used to itinerant workers arriving in late Spring and leaving in early Autumn. As the daylight hours shrank and people turned their backs on Summer frivolities and looked out their warm winter clothing, they were mindful of saving up for Christmas treats for their families.

But there were many weeks to go before the holiday season would end. And who knew what this Englishman would have to say to him? Patrik grinned as he lifted his face to the warm sunshine. Maybe he should have consulted Madame Clara, the fortune teller whose tent he'd noticed at the other end of the fairground, away from the noisiest rides. But that would have meant crossing the lady's palm with silver and Patrik knew he must save every single bit of that he possibly could.

"Good morning, Patrik. I hope I haven't kept you waiting."

Patrik got off the low stone wall and stood to attention. "No, sir. I mean, Charlie. I wish you a very good morning too."

"Let's go and have breakfast. I...um ... I was a bit late on parade this morning so I could do with a nice big plate of eggs and bacon. I'll explain why I asked you to meet me, while we eat. That sound good to you?"

Bonnie with her mother and Kay were always extra-busy on changeover day. With the exception of the honeymoon suite, they'd stripped off all the guest beds and Diane's much-appreciated washing machine was rumbling and whooshing while she and the girls shined up washbasins and replaced all of the used bed linen with fresh, lavender-scented sheets and pillow-cases. At the sound of the doorbell, Diane hurried downstairs to let the police in while the two girls continued with their chores.

"I hope they won't want to interview us," Bonnie said as she and Kay worked on their hospital corners in one of the sea-facing guest rooms.

"Me too. I wouldn't know what to say about Mr and Mrs White. Apart from the usual asking how they'd like their eggs cooked and wishing them a lovely day, I know nothing at all about them."

"I had a peep in the guest book to see what the husband wrote and the address is clearly written but I imagine it's a made up one. Mum says the room booking was made over the 'phone and she received a postal order as a deposit. No clues there, then."

"So now they've done a runner, the police have no way of knowing where the couple are heading. Did they travel by train?" Kay asked.

"No. They came by car. If not, they couldn't have gone anywhere as there are no buses or trains or taxis at three in the morning."

"How do you know what time they went?"

"As it happens, Mum woke around three a.m. and she told me she heard a faint noise but assumed it must have been someone getting out of bed to use the toilet," Bonnie said, straightening up. "Right, that's this bed looking shipshape."

"But the honeymoon suite has its own little bathroom." Kay was frowning.

"Mum heard the sound of a door closing quietly though it could've been made by any of the guests. She doesn't get out of bed to investigate, every time she hears someone moving round in the small hours."

"No, of course she doesn't." Kay sighed. "I must tell your mum to dock some money from my wages today. I feel so sorry for her, being duped like that."

Bonnie felt a rush of gratitude. "That's very thoughtful of you, but I'm sure Mum won't expect you to go short because of one couple's dishonesty."

"Well, your mum's always very kind to me. Goodness, it's a pity she can't lock the front and back doors at night and take the keys to her room with her!"

Bonnie chuckled. "It's a thought, but it's not the best of ideas. What if there should be a fire?"

Kay shuddered. "Heaven forbid! It was terrifying enough when fire broke out at the fairground. Waking up to find the house ablaze would be ...oh, I don't want to think about it, Bonnie!"

"Well, Mum's made sure all the rooms have a polite notice requesting guests not to smoke, so let's hope nothing awful ever happens." She checked her watch. "Could I leave you to polish the furniture and use the carpet sweeper? I need to check whether the washing's ready to hang out."

"Of course. And maybe we can have a chat about Jack and Patrik. Jack seems fine with Patrik, so it might be nice to arrange a foursome some time."

Bonnie couldn't help feeling a little indignant. Patrik was a fellow funfair employee and he was as responsible for the holidaymakers' safety as Jack Williams was. Kay made it sound as though Jack was the one who decided whether Patrik should be allowed to join them or not. But she knew how thrilled her friend was to be going out with her former boyfriend again and she was far too fond of Kay to make a fuss.

"Well, it's going to be difficult as they both work evenings, but maybe we can fix something up if that's what you'd like."

Kay was already polishing the big walnut wardrobe. She turned to face her friend. "Are you saying you don't want us to double date? You want to keep Patrik all to yourself? Does this mean you're serious about him?"

Bonnie shook her head so vigorously, she needed to

smooth down her blonde curls. "First of all, you tell me to beware of making friends with a Hungarian boy, now you're asking me whether Patrik and I are going steady! What's made you change your mind?"

"Several things, in fact."

"OK. I need to get that washing out as it's a lovely, breezy morning. Let's finish this conversation later, shall we?"

She was on her way through the door when she heard her mother call from the bottom of the stairs. "Bonnie? Kay? Could you come downstairs, please. Sergeant Jones would like to ask you a few questions."

"I'll be mother, shall I?"

Patrik looked at Charlie Hamilton in bemusement. "So sorry. I thought I hear you say you will be mother."

Charlie roared with laughter. "Sorry, I didn't think. It's an expression we use about the person who's pouring the tea for everyone else."

"Ah. I see now. Yes, it is good expression." Patrik accepted a cup.

"And here come our breakfasts. Dig in, Patrik."

"That is expression I hear before." Patrik regarded the plateful of food with awe. Back home, this portion would have fed three people. He couldn't help feeling guilty, but his brother had advised him not to look back to things he couldn't control, but to look to the future and accept any opportunities coming his way. He couldn't wait to hear what this man wearing a smart business suit had to say to him. He didn't need to wait long.

"Patrik, as I already told you, I work as a sales representative, but through my business contacts, I've been lucky enough to find alternative ways of making money. Do you understand what I'm saying?"

"It is other ways of making money than by selling to the gift shops?"

Charlie beamed and speared a sausage. "Exactly. My, shall we say, second business, is all to do with high-quality goods. Not any old cheap tin whistles and baubles, but the really luxurious items like gold watches and pearl necklaces."

Patrik nodded. "Superior to the mass market things."

"Good man. Have you been having English lessons?"

"No, sir. I listen to the radio when I can. And if I find newspaper lying around, I take it away to read later." Suddenly he felt worried. "Is not against Great Britain's laws, I hope?"

"'Course not. You've got your head screwed on. You're using your noddle!" Charlie laughed at sight of the young Hungarian's puzzlement. "Both those expressions mean you're intelligent and using your brain to work things out for yourself. I'm sure you're the right person to help me with my second business." He put down his knife and fork and leaned forward. "On the condition that you say nothing to anyone about it. Get it? You keep your mouth shut and do as you're told and you'll end up with a nice lump of commission to put in your post office savings bank."

"I have not got one of those. Not sure I am allowed. I give my saved money to my brother. I have great trust in Istvan."

"Ah. OK. I'll find out about opening you a savings account. We wouldn't want Istvan to wonder where your extra money is coming from, now would we?"

Patrik's turn to put down his cutlery and lean forward. "I understand this is secret operation, but I tell my brother everything."

"Not this time, I'm afraid. No offence to your

brother, but I don't want people to know I have, let's say, a second string to my bow. I already have a driver, but now and then he needs someone with him to help shift goods. Open doors and so on. Get it?"

"I get it."

"Can you drive? I forgot to ask."

"I used to drive my father's car but here I have no licence."

"That can be sorted, as long as you know what you're doing behind the wheel."

Charlie topped up their teacups. "Don't look so worried, Patrik. A lot of fellows round here would jump at the chance to earn some extra cash, but I've chosen you to help me because I know you have a good brain and you're eager to make something of yourself. But it's important you don't say a word about any of this to those people you live with or to your brother and his mates. I need to be absolutely certain you understand that, before I tell you anything more."

Patrik finished his mouthful of egg and bacon. He wanted very much to trust this man. He had become very good at keeping secrets back in his own country and now he desperately needed some way of strengthening his position in his new country. "Yes, sir. I understand."

"Good man. Now, what's the situation between you and young Bonnie?"

Patrik pictured Bonnie in her brightly-coloured skirt and white blouse. She had beautiful golden hair and a sweet smile. He wanted to make her feel proud of him, but how could she do that while he remained a worker on a fairground ride?

"I wait for her to come to see me. I know where she lives, but I think it is not respectful for me to call at her mother's house."

"Very wise. I knew I'd chosen the right man for the

work I have in mind."

They ate in silence for a while. Patrik longed to find out more about this mysterious business he was about to become involved with, but experience told him to wait for the other person to take the lead.

Charlie leaned forward and spoke in a low voice. "I'll need you with me tomorrow night when I drive to the airport. I shan't bother Ken this time. He's my regular driver, but as I'd like to show you the ropes, I'll drive you. Can you be ready at nine o'clock if I pick you up near your caravan?"

"I must tell you where to find me."

"No need. I make it my business to know these things. You share with three other pleasure park workers, don't you? The caravan's on that waste ground just around the point."

Patrik nodded, his thoughts whirling. He would ask the other young man who worked with him on the Spanish Waltzer. Their boss calculated when he needed both of them on duty at the same time, but they sometimes swapped shifts that covered the quieter periods and Patrik's workmate was usually the one asking for a favour.

"I need to change my shift. How can I get message to you?"

"I'll drop by the ride on my way back later. Will you be there at about half-past five?" He paused. "If you can't manage it, maybe I'll need to rethink my offer of work ..."

Patrik didn't like to think of missing what might be a golden opportunity. "I'm sure I can arrange things. Leave it with me, please."

Charlie Hamilton nodded. "We'll wait and see." He drained his teacup and pushed back his chair. "Right then, I'll settle up and be on my way. Until later then,

Patrik."

The young Hungarian nodded his thanks and rose too. Well aware he was putting himself in a vulnerable position, he asked himself whether he could truly trust this Englishman. But he had the strong feeling that it wouldn't be wise to back out now.

CHAPTER 6

"Did you ever notice Mr and Mrs White chatting with other guests, Miss Morgan?"

Bonnie wrinkled her brow as she thought. The police sergeant had stressed the possible importance of every little detail. "I don't think so," she said at last. "But I suppose honeymooners prefer each other's company." She hoped she didn't blush.

The officer continued looking down at his notes. "Hmm, that tallies with what your mother and Miss Smith have said. Did you ever see either of the couple on their own outside the guest house? Down on the prom for instance."

"Not once," she said. "The only time I saw them outside of the house was last night and they were definitely together. I was walking back from the funfair with ...with a friend." At once she regretted her words. Patrik shouldn't be dragged into this.

"And did you or your friend speak to them?"

"No. Mr and Mrs White had their arms around each other as they were walking and I didn't notice either of them looking round. They were far enough ahead of us for me not to notice them at first."

"What made you look at them then, Miss Morgan?"

"Nothing. I suddenly realised they were two of our guests. Mrs White is the same height as her husband, so

I think that's what made me realise who they were."

"You mentioned being out with a friend. Did this friend of yours ever visit the guest house and meet Mr and Mrs White?"

"Definitely not. My friend is someone I met only recently and he's never been inside our house."

She saw the officer raise his eyebrows. *Please*, Bonnie agonised. *Oh, please don't ask questions about Patrik.* She still wasn't sure how secure the young refugee's position might be. Bonnie wished for something to fan her hot cheeks with. The officer had insisted on closing the dining room window, for security purposes he'd said. In case of eavesdroppers.

"I see," he said at last. "When was the last time you saw Mr and Mrs White, Miss Morgan?"

"That would be last night as I was returning home. We didn't realise they'd left until this morning when Kay knocked on the door and took in their tea."

"And during their stay, did you ever see anything, shall we say unusual, while you were going about your duties in their room?"

"Nothing at all. We don't make a habit of looking in guests' suitcases or rummaging in drawers and wardrobes." She lifted her chin.

He cleared his throat. "Quite so. Well, should you recall anything, no matter how trivial, which you think might help our inquiries, please let me know, miss."

"I will. Is that all you need from me now, Officer?"

"Yes, thank you." He tapped his pencil against his cheek. "You should understand there's a strong possibility that the couple in question very probably gave you an assumed name. On looking at your guest book, the address one of them wrote isn't known to our colleagues in the Essex Constabulary. But the description your mother gave us tallies with something we have on record. Whether or not our inquiries will bear fruit is debatable, but should we hear anything, we shall of course inform you."

"We shouldn't get our hopes up, I suppose." Bonnie grimaced. "This makes me wish I could give a description of Mr and Mrs White to everyone running a hotel or guest house."

"Indeed. We will in due course be issuing a statement which will be issued to the BBC and the national press. If, as we suspect, Mr and Mrs White have pulled the same trick elsewhere, then others in your position should contact their local police station and this may well enable us to build up a dossier on the couple. We may find a pattern in their movement. Time will tell."

Before the police officer left, he gave Mrs Morgan the go ahead for the honeymoon suite to be cleaned and prepared for its next occupants. Diane asked Bonnie and Kay to work together on Room 1 after they completed their other chores.

Bonnie entered the bedroom first and stood inside, looking round her, wrinkling her nose in annoyance. "What a state to leave a room in," she said as Kay came through the door. "All the drawers left open and the wardrobe doors. Bedding pulled off and dumped on the floor, including that beautiful blue satin eiderdown. Those coppers are a messy lot!"

"I expect that young constable who was here was told to be as quick as he could," Kay said. "I've heard about the police turning a place upside down when they make a search. Though this is isn't what I'd call a crime scene."

"That's all very well, but this isn't my idea of how to make a thorough search. Flinging stuff about that that!

I wouldn't be surprised if he was imagining himself as the detective in one of those crime films. Kay, would you mind collecting all the bed linen very carefully, please? Could you turn the pillow cases inside out and once the bed's stripped, check around the mattress to make sure nothing's fallen down?"

"Yes, if that's what you want. But do you really think we might find something when the police haven't?"

"Kay, I don't know, but I think we should be more thorough than that young officer probably has. At least, if we find nothing suspicious, we'll have the satisfaction of knowing we had a jolly good try."

Bonnie walked across to the bathroom. The door stood open and towels had been flung on the floor. She picked each one up and folded it neatly, ready to be added to the next batch for washing. Next, she looked inside the small wall cabinet which was always left empty and wiped out for the room's next occupants. Sometimes, it was surprising how people forgot to collect items they'd left in there, but today the shelves were empty. Then she checked the washbasin and toilet areas, kneeling, so she could feel around the back of each. Nothing was revealed, though she knew her mother would be pleased at the absence of dust, proving neither of her assistants lacked in thoroughness.

She called to Kay that she was about to start cleaning, but her friend appeared in the doorway, holding a small piece of paper in the palm of one hand.

"Ooh, what have you got there?" Bonnie asked.

Kay passed it to her. "It looks as though it's been torn from a small notebook. Read it and tell me what you think."

Bonnie read aloud, "Walton Towers, Linden Avenue, Beckchester. Goodness, this sounds like a posh place to me. I wonder whether that couple stayed there before coming here, or is this where they might be heading after leaving us?"

"Intriguing, isn't it?"

"Where did you find this?"

"Down beneath the bedhead and behind the mattress."

"Well done, Kay. Your chambermaiding skills have come in useful in more ways than one."

"Thanks, but this is down to you for deciding to make another search."

"Somehow, I knew we'd find something. It might be nothing significant but I'll take it down to Mum so she can ring that sergeant. I could drop it round to the police station this afternoon in my free time."

"Good thinking. I've promised to go and keep an eye on my gran after I finish here, so I don't plan on visiting the pleasure park. Will you be going to see Patrik while you're out?" Kay's eyes sparkled.

"Whatever makes you ask that, Miss Smith?"

"The fact that I know you so well, Miss Morgan. You may deny it, but I know you've fallen for a certain young Hungarian. So there!"

While Diane Morgan was at the hairdresser's, getting glammed up as her daughter described it, Bonnie and Kay continued their chores and discussed the agonising dilemma of liking a boy, wanting to keep him interested, but not wanting him to feel he was being chased.

It was almost three o'clock by the time Diane returned from her hairdo, her fair hair swept into an elegant chignon. With her mother there to welcome new arrivals, Bonnie was able to take a break, but firstly she walked to the police station where she handed over the 'evidence' as the constable on the desk described it. Once outside again, she was trying to decide whether to wander along to the pleasure park or not. The beach was always busy on high season weekends while the funfair usually came fully to life in the evenings when holidaymakers packed away their buckets and spades and sought a more challenging kind of entertainment.

Bonnie's mum had asked her to be back by five thirty to allow herself plenty of time to get ready for the dinner dance. This wasn't a problem for Bonnie as Diane hardly ever went out of an evening and most guests who arrived late afternoon were keen to unpack their cases and go straight out to explore. Sometimes guests who returned to the bay year after year, appreciated a pot of tea and a chat with the proprietor, but this week the only returners booked in had arrived early afternoon and were already out.

Bonnie opted for a walk along the promenade and through the municipal gardens over at the other side of the bay. Her attention was caught by the sound of raucous squawky voices and laughter and she turned to look down at the sands where the regular Punch and Judy man had set up his distinctive striped canvas booth. Smiling at the familiar sight which she hadn't seen since last August, Bonnie stopped to watch the action.

Poor, woebegone Judy! she thought. As usual, she was having a hard time with Punch, though the audience were loving every minute of the knockabout show. Why were kids so bloodthirsty?

She was about to move on when she noticed a man walking down the slope towards the beach. He headed along the sand and she frowned, wondering what he was doing down there, looking so out of place in his dark, business suit. Instinctively, Bonnie drew back, in case he should glance up and spot her. She had no idea why she did this but was intrigued as Mr Hamilton could only have come to see the show, but how very strange was that? She glanced at her wrist watch and realised he had plenty of time to return to the guest house and get changed for the dinner dance.

After a while, she decided she was being silly and almost went on her way, but with the performance coming to a noisy end and the audience clapping and cheering, Hamilton showed no sign of leaving. As people moved away, he walked round to the back of the booth, disappearing from her view. Curiouser and curiouser ...

A minute or two later, he came back into sight, though still close to the booth and with the Punch and Judy man beside him. Bonnie saw him reach for his briefcase, take what looked like an envelope from it, then hand it to the other man while exchanging a quick word with him, before striding across the soft sand towards the ramp leading to the prom.

Swiftly, Bonnie set off again, deliberately not looking over her shoulder. It would be awful if he thought she'd been spying on him, even if it was true, but only because it seemed so strange to see their regular guest down on the beach when he usually relied upon the retailers and amusement arcade owners for trade. She was certain the Punch and Judy man never gave away prizes during his shows.

Bonnie spotted an empty bench overlooking the sea and made her way over to it, sitting down to watch the progress of a pleasure steamer heading back with passengers wanting to disembark at the pier. She couldn't help thinking of the businessman's behaviour earlier that day when he seemed so anxious not to be around when the police called. What could he possibly have to be worried about? Surely... surely, he couldn't be involved in shady dealings? Her heart bumped a little faster as she thought about her mother and whether she should tell her what she'd seen.

"Penny for 'em!"

Startled, Bonnie looked up. The object of her puzzlement stood there, smiling. Casting a long, narrow shadow and holding his briefcase, he was, she thought, quite a good-looking man, although, in her opinion he used too much hair cream.

"Mind if I join you?"

Before she could say a word, he sat down beside her.

CHAPTER 7

"That was an unpleasant thing to happen to your mother, wasn't it?"

"Yes, and it's upsetting for us all, Mr Hamilton." Bonnie continued gazing at the pleasure steamer which was docking at the pier. Seagulls, ever-hopeful, were hovering round its bows, hoping for leftover titbits to be flung into the water.

"Of course, and do call me Charlie. Let's hope the boys in blue can track the couple down."

For some reason, Bonnie didn't feel inclined to tell him about the piece of paper she'd found bearing information which might or might not prove useful to the police.

"I'm sure they'll do their best," she said.

"I'm sorry you'll be spending the evening at home, Bonnie. A pretty girl like you should be out having fun on a Saturday night, dancing and spending time with friends. It seemed a good opportunity to give your mother a break from routine, but I realise it means you have to stay in."

"It's not a problem. We're a team, my mother, Kay and me."

"A very good team too, though it still can't be easy, making time to see that young man of yours. What was his name again?"

Bonnie was beginning to feel irritated. She glanced at her watch and got to her feet. But her natural politeness plus the determination not to upset one of her mother's regular guests, made her hesitate.

"Forgive me, Mr Hamilton, but I'd like to finish my walk now. I don't want to make my mother late for her appointment with you."

Charlie grinned. "That's put me in my place. Don't get me wrong, but I wouldn't want to see you getting hurt."

"Why should I get hurt? I take it you're warning me about Patrik Matyaz?" She stopped herself from telling him it was none of his business who she saw in her free time.

"These itinerant workers come and go, my dear. It's part of their nature. I'm not against them, please don't think that. But a young man from such an unsettled background can't possibly hold the same values as someone from your own class. I'm sure your mum would say he isn't good enough for you."

"Whatever you say, Mr Hamilton." Bonnie didn't want to be his dear and she felt too angry to stand there any longer. If she did, she wouldn't be able to stop herself from telling this man exactly what she thought of his unwanted opinions, especially about class. She suspected Patrik came from a more superior background then Charlie did.

"Enjoy your evening out and forgive me if I don't wait up!" With that, she set off, intent on walking on for another ten minutes before turning back.

On her way home, Bonnie decided there'd be no harm in taking a short cut through the pleasure park. She and Kay had been doing that for years and if she happened to see Patrik, and he wasn't too busy, she could stop to say a quick hello. Bonnie enjoyed walking through the funfair, listening to the songs playing from different areas as she passed, and seeing the children's delighted faces always cheered her up if she was feeling a bit down.

Why, she wondered, did she have this uneasy feeling about Charlie Hamilton who had stayed so many times in the guesthouse? If that couple hadn't left like they did, there would have been no need to call the police. No need for Charlie to behave in a suspicious manner, almost as though he was afraid of being asked questions. Did he have something to hide?

Bonnie sighed and lifted her face to the sun, enjoying its warmth. On approaching the rear entrance to the pleasure park, she immediately heard the sound of one of her favourite pop songs, *Love Letters in the Sand*, sung by Pat Boone. She smiled to herself as she remembered Kay declaring how she'd like to marry the handsome singer. No doubt she'd changed her mind now she was seeing twinkly-eyed Jack the mechanic again.

Bonnie walked past people rolling coloured balls down a gently sloping surface, aiming for the openings with the highest numbers painted on them. But the hidden twists and turns invisible to the eye made for unexpected results and not many people scored as well as they tried to. It occurred to her how much this game resembled life.

She barely glanced at the Wall of Death looming up on her left, but looked back at once, hoping she'd been mistaken with what she saw. To her dismay, one of the mechanics, unmissable in his blue dungarees, was standing near the payment kiosk, in deep conversation with a pretty brunette. The mechanic was her friend's boyfriend and, much to Bonnie's dismay, he was with a girl who'd been at school with both Bonnie and Kay.

How many more secrets would she be obliged to

hide? Bonnie ducked into the nearest amusement arcade and pretended to study one of the slot machines. The one she chose required sixpence to be inserted before the mechanism operated. A claw on the end of a metal arm would then swoop around the glass-fronted cabinet, before dipping to snap its jaws closed, whether they contained a prize or not. These were mainly gaudy bangles, cheap necklaces and children's toys with one or two fluffy bears thrown in as an extra incentive to try your luck. She suspected they might be supplied by Mr Charlie Hamilton.

"Excuse me, darlin'. Are you going to have a go at this, or not?"

Bonnie looked round to find a man waiting, holding a small girl's hand. "I'm so sorry," she said. "I'll get out of your way."

She walked across the arcade and left without a second glance at Jack and his companion. There might, she told herself, be a logical explanation. But although she tried to find some excuse like both of them living in the same road and being just friends, the more she pictured how closely the two had stood together. Worse still, how the girl had looked up at Jack so adoringly as he talked to her.

Bonnie wanted nothing more now than to get home. Far above her one of the scenic railway cars rumbled along, its passengers screaming either with delight or fright. She was almost at the Spanish Waltzer when she stopped in her tracks, caught as she remembered being once caught by her mum, as she climbed on to the kitchen cabinet, her small fingers reaching for the biscuit tin before a pair of arms hugged her and lifted her away.

That was a faraway childhood memory. But this was now and no childish prank. She went on walking. But here was another pair. Yet again two people she knew. This time, Patrik stood, eyes fixed on his companion, concentrating hard on what the older man was saying. From time to time, the young Hungarian nodded his head as his companion issued whatever advice or instructions he was giving. For sure, this was no friendly chit chat arising because Charlie Hamilton happened to be visiting a customer nearby.

Bonnie felt a little light-headed and the sensation had nothing to do with the combined smells of frying onions and sweet, sticky candy floss. She took a deep breath, doing her best to melt into a crowd of holidaymakers wandering by, laughing and joking and wearing *Kiss me Quick* hats. What was wrong with everyone? What in the world could Charlie Hamilton want with Patrik? And should she warn Kay to be wary of becoming too involved with Jack Williams? If he really was two-timing her friend, you'd think he'd have the common sense not to hang around with a girl in such a public place. Kay was spending time with her grandmother that afternoon as the old lady wasn't very well and the family were rallying around. But what could Jack be thinking of, behaving like this? When she left her gran's house, Kay might well drop by the ride now she and Jack were supposedly close once more.

At the thought of witnessing such a confrontation, and determined to avoid either Patrik or his companion noticing her, Bonnie hurried through the happy throng of people. She needed time to think things through. But what a strange day this was turning out to be.

Bonnie found her mother in her bedroom, wearing a floral housecoat and blowing on her newly-varnished glossy pink nails.

"Did you enjoy your walk, love?"

"Um, yes. It was fine, Mum. Is there anything you need me to know before you go out?"

"Three couples have already checked in and gone out again. The family who booked two rooms aren't due to arrive until about seven. You could offer them a pot of tea, I suppose."

"Of course. What about Room 1? That's reserved as well, isn't it?"

"Yes. Not honeymooners this time, but a pleasant couple from Oxford who stayed with us a couple of summers back. The husband decided to book the same room as a surprise for his wife. A bouquet of red roses was delivered for her after you went out. Isn't that romantic? I put them in the best vase I could find and they're already scenting the room."

"Lovely. Right, so six have arrived and six are still to come. Don't worry. I'll look after everyone, so you just go and have a good time."

"Thanks, Bonnie. By the way, you haven't seen my eternity ring anywhere, have you? I must have put it down somewhere, I suppose, but it's annoying because I wanted to wear it this evening."

Bonnie shook her head. "Sorry, Mum. I'd have brought it to you if I'd noticed it anywhere. Are you sure it isn't in your jewel box?"

"It's not there, which means I've definitely left it somewhere else. I'll check the kitchen window sill when I go downstairs. It wouldn't be the first time I've put it down and forgotten it."

Bonnie nodded. "I hope it hasn't fallen down somewhere. I'll go and check for you. I know you like to wear it for special occasions."

"Thanks, lovey." Diane hesitated. "I'm under no illusions about Charlie, you know. If you ask me, he had some other lady lined up to attend this dance with him and whoever it was let him down at the last minute. I'm probably his second or third choice."

Bonnie couldn't help feeling relief. "Well, I'm glad you're not serious about him, Mum."

"He's pleasant enough. And it'll be a change to get dressed up for once." She glanced at the clock. "Speaking of which, I must get into my party frock. There's a ham salad in the pantry for you, Bonnie. And the remains of that apple pie Kay made yesterday."

Bonnie was about to thank her when the doorbell rang.

"I'll go! You need to be ready for your escort." Bonnie set off downstairs, her welcoming smile in place ready to greet the young couple who stood inside the porch, holding hands, their cases beside them.

"Mr and Mrs Grant? I remember you from last year. Do come in."

Bonnie had greeted so many guests, both new ones and those who'd stayed before, that she found it easy to make conversation with strangers or with people she couldn't recall meeting. On this occasion, it was a huge relief to forget the unwelcome and puzzling happenings this day had brought. But there were unresolved issues that she knew wouldn't vanish quite so fast as the slice of apple pie she looked forward to later.

Saturday night meant the busiest night of the week for those working on the pleasure park. In between selling tickets and making sure his riders were safely fastened into the cars, then released when the ride ground to a halt, Patrik couldn't stop thinking about the position he found himself in. He simply couldn't make up his mind whether he felt excited or apprehensive – a word he'd only just learned – regarding the possibility of becoming some sort of assistant to Mr Hamilton. As thing were, his pay packet wouldn't stretch to asking Bonnie to join him on an evening out. Free evenings were rare anyway. But the only chance of earning enough cash to take her to a good restaurant meant giving up yet more of his limited free time. It seemed late nights would be involved, so Patrik's hours of sleep would be cut short.

There had been no sign of Bonnie since he'd walked her home on Friday evening, but what did he expect? She was busy too. She'd explained Saturdays meant extra work as most bookings were for seven nights, after which guests left and new ones arrived. That meant lots of washing and lots of cleaning. No wonder such a pretty girl didn't already have a boy-friend. He respected her for being so loyal to her mother, but although she'd seemed to enjoy his company well enough, he sensed something about Bonnie which made him wonder if she trusted him well enough for them to spend more time together.

How could he blame her? After all, he was a foreigner, living in temporary accommodation while estranged from his own country and lacking the qualifications which he felt sure Bonnie's mother would wish any potential boy-friend of her daughter to hold.

Around eight o'clock, Patrik looked up to see Jack from the Wall of Death walking towards him, hand in hand with a pretty dark-haired girl. He wore a sports jacket and striped shirt with slacks, so obviously wasn't working that evening. Patrik felt puzzled and wondered how Jack could have been so friendly towards Bonnie's friend Kay the evening before, then turn up next day with a different girl. But he knew better than to show his feelings, so smiled in his friend's direction and gave him a wave.

As he waited for the mechanic to reach the Spanish Waltzer, the girl left Jack's side and ran across to one of the booths lining the concourse.

Jack grinned as he arrived. "Hiya, mate!" He nodded towards the booths. "Jenny has a pal working on the Ring the Duck stall. It's a good job she told me – I don't want to be seen out with Kay and have someone tell Jenny about my other girlfriend, now do I?"

Patrik felt horrified, but attempted a smile. "Or the other way around?" he suggested.

Jack nodded. "You're not joking. That'd probably put Kay off me for ever. We used to go out together when we first left school but it didn't work out. We were only kids back then. Now I'd really like to give it another chance."

"So sorry, Jack, but I wonder why you go out with two young ladies in that case. Why you risk losing Kay? What if she comes to funfair and sees you with another girl?"

"Good question. But Kay and I only got together again yesterday. I've been seeing Jenny for a few weeks now, but the moment I saw Kay again, something clicked, and I knew I must stop seeing Jenny." He glanced across at the booth where she stood talking. "Don't say a word of this to Bonnie, mind. I need to finish with Jenny tonight, but I'll take her for a Knickerbocker Glory and some coffee first, then break the news gently."

"What is Knickerbocker Glory?" Whatever it was, Patrik hoped it would be less complicated than Jack's love life.

"Mate, you haven't lived if you haven't tasted one of those! As long as you like vanilla ice-cream and fruit and whipped cream. Mind you, they cost half-a-crown, so be warned."

Patrik noticed Jenny start walking back to Jack. "You better go talk with your girl. And please believe I say nothing to any person."

Judging by the angry expression on the young lady's face, the Hungarian thought Jack's fears of being found out might be about to be realised.

CHAPTER 8

Bonnie was curled up on the sofa in her mother's private room, reading a library book. Right from the start, she'd loved Dodie Smith's novel, *I Capture the Castle* and only wished she could fit more reading into her busy days. She wondered what her mother would do when she eventually found a job, which she hoped to achieve in September. The guest house was open for business all year round and even when there weren't many guests staying, there always seemed more than enough for one person to do. But there were friends Diane could call on and, Bonnie thought as she heard the doorbell ring, Kay might like some extra hours while deciding what job she would really like to do.

She glanced at her watch as she walked down the hallway. Her mother had her key with her and besides, it was far too early to expect her and her escort home. The other guests were either in their rooms or relaxing in the residents' lounge.

Having opened the front door, Bonnie was surprised to see her best friend standing in the porchway.

"I need a word. Can I come in?" Kay's expression was woebegone to say the least, and Bonnie thought her eyes looked suspiciously red.

"Of course! We'll go through to the kitchen. You look as though you could do with a hot drink."

Kay followed Bonnie into the kitchen and closed the door behind them before the floodgates opened.

"I can't help it!" she sobbed. "It's so awful. Why do I have such bad luck with Jack? I can't believe he'd two-time me again, Bonnie. What do you think?" She sniffed loudly and wiped her nose with her hand.

Apparently, the worst must have happened, but Bonnie needed time to think. She reached for a pristine linen handkerchief from a pile of folded laundry. "Here, mop up with this. Tea or coffee?"

"T...tea, please." Kay blew her nose and settled into the nearest chair, clutching the white handkerchief like an unhappy toddler reaching for her comfort blanket.

"I was thinking about having a piece of that apple pie you made." Bonnie filled the kettle and lit the gas hob. "Shall I cut two slices?"

"Just tea will be fine, thanks. I'm so sorry to barge in like this, but I couldn't bear to go home feeling like I do. And I know your mum won't be back from her night out yet."

At that moment, Bonnie wanted nothing more than to tell Jack Williams exactly what she thought of him. She'd never seen her friend look so wretched. It seemed what Bonnie feared had indeed happened. Jack deserved to be found out but this was very hard on Kay, who appeared to have fallen suddenly and joyfully in love with a young man who still had so much to learn about loyalty and life in general. She dreaded the thought of telling her best friend she'd seen Jack with another girl, but decided to hold her tongue.

Bonnie sat down beside Kay while she waited for the tea to brew. Her friend was sitting up straight now.

"Of course, it might only be gossip," Kay said. "Now I think about it, that girl who works shifts on the Ring the Duck stall could've been trying to cause mischief because she wants Jack for herself. Some girls would do anything to get a boyfriend. What do you think?"

Bonnie tried to take this in. She didn't want to dash her friend's hopes, nor did she intend being unrealistic. "Um, how did you come to be talking to that girl? I know who you mean but I don't know her name."

"She didn't go to our school because she's not long moved here. She told me that when we were both queuing for the toilets down at the funfair."

Bonnie frowned. "Did you know her already? Or d'you mean you just got chatting?"

"She lives across the road from my gran and she's seen me going in and out of Gran's house. There's a girl called Jenny living two doors up. You might remember her from school and this new girl has got friendly with Jenny and she told me Jack from the Wall of Death is seeing Jenny. That means he's been two-timing me. Already!"

Bonnie began pouring the tea. Maybe there was a way to ease Kay's heartache, even if only temporarily. After all, she needn't tell her friend she'd seen Jack with Jenny. Not saying anything wouldn't be lying and there could still be some simple explanation, though she wished she didn't keep remembering Jenny's obvious admiration for Jack. It seemed on the cards one of these two smitten girls might be heading for heartbreak.

"Let me get this straight. You haven't actually seen Jack with Jenny, but you believe what this other girl is saying? Come on, Kay! I bet you're right and this is something made up and intended to put you off him. You and Jack have only just got together again, for goodness' sake."

Kay picked up her cup, took a sip of tea and hiccupped. She heaved a sigh and dabbed at her nose. "I want to believe you. I don't want to believe Jack would hurt me, but that girl sounded so convincing."

"That's what troublemakers thrive on. Convincing you something's true because they want you to believe it is." Bonnie dug into her slice of apple pie. "I know how I'd handle this, but you may not feel the same."

"Tell me what you'd do then."

"When are you due to see Jack next?"

"Tomorrow night. He wants to take me to the flicks to see *Ill Met by Moonlight*. It's showing at the Roxy."

"Dirk Bogarde's lush! OK, so tell me how Jack can afford to take you to the cinema, probably buy you a choc ice as well, then do the same with another girl?"

Kay took another sip of tea. "Put like that, it does seem unlikely. Except, I wouldn't put it past his mother to be still giving him pocket money. But I was caught off guard and remembering how he suddenly finished with me that time when we'd only just left school, I suppose I jumped to conclusions."

Bonnie felt she was still walking on shifting sands. She wondered whether she should corner Jack without delay. Make sure he truly wasn't seeing both girls at once. If that was the case, she'd also advise him to have a word with Beaky – as she'd privately christened the girl from the Ring the Duck stall – though it wasn't in her nature to be cruel in any way. If Jack was playing fast and loose, Bonnie wanted to make sure she frightened the daylights out of him. If he turned out to be a liar, her friend would be well rid of him. But try telling that to Kay now!

Patrik wanted to see Bonnie again. Except, that didn't describe his true feelings. More than anything else in the world, he longed to be with her. Already it seemed an age since she'd dropped a goodnight kiss on his cheek. Yet, if he did meet her, he'd find it difficult not to confide in her about the new job he'd been offered. He dared not risk upsetting Mr Hamilton because, without some means of earning extra cash, Patrik doubted he had any hope of becoming Bonnie's boyfriend. Apart from his brother, Istvan, and the three fairground workers with whom he shared the caravan, Jack Williams was the only other young man Patrik spent time with, and his relationship with the Wall of Death mechanic was nothing like true friendship. Not like the bond he'd shared with his late friend, Luca.

But he mustn't keep looking back. He must view the past as a series of events which helped shape him and make him stronger. Although many of his experiences had been tragic, frightening and at the very least worrying, he knew he'd learnt many things the hard way. Already he was beginning to love his new country. He didn't want to put a foot wrong. And, if he should succeed in winning the heart of the prettiest, nicest young lady he'd met in his life so far, either in Hungary or Wales, he would make sure not to play fast and loose with her feelings.

Patrick felt Jack was risking trouble. Rekindling a former romance was all very well, but surely you didn't do that while still involved with a present one? Patrik's struggle to find the right English word to describe Jack, led him to ask his boss at the Waltzer for suggestions. The boss had told Patrik whoever it was must be a fool, declaring one girl was trouble enough, especially if she was pretty, without becoming involved with two of the little minxes!

His young employee decided to leave the fine-tuning of his English language skills to another occasion and under no circumstances would he mention anything to Bonnie. He would respect Jack's wishes as he would respect Mr Hamilton's instructions. He wasn't exactly sure what 'keeping schtum' meant, but he figured it must have something to do with holding his tongue. Best not to ask Mr Hamilton and risk – what was it Jack had said when talking about work? Something about taking care not to drop himself in it.

A trio of teenage girls were paying for their tickets at the kiosk. Patrik was fastening safety bars. When he reached the car containing the three young ladies, he gave them his usual smile. Sometimes girls would ask what his name was and when he told them, they usually assumed he was British, unless they managed to keep him talking. Before Bonnie entered his life so unexpectedly, he'd had no wish to begin a relationship. After all, what could he offer? And he wasn't interested in the kind of girls who hung around the rides, eyeing up the young men working there.

Sometimes, on hearing his accent, the riders would look the other way or begin talking amongst themselves. Patrik had become used to this and luckily it didn't happen very often. When it did, he consoled himself by thinking of the beautiful golden-haired girl who had bumped into him what seemed an age ago. She was different from any other girl he'd ever known. But that momentous meeting happened not long ago. He would be patient. He would do as everyone wanted him to do. And if he obeyed orders and pleased Mr Hamilton, maybe things would begin to go his way. More than anything else, Patrik longed to hold his head high and make Bonnie proud to be his friend.

But the anxiety rumbling in his tummy every time he thought of what might lie ahead wasn't easy to banish.

CHAPTER 9

Bonnie thought Kay was feeling better by the time her friend left *Sea Breezes* to walk home before nightfall. Tomorrow, when Kay met Jack for their cinema date, she would need to ask him if there was any truth in the rumour she'd heard.

Bonnie had remembered to ask Kay if she'd noticed Diane's ring anywhere, but sadly her friend was also unable to help. Bonnie washed up the tea things, answered the door to the returning family of four and chatted to them for a while, before returning to her library book. It was almost eleven o'clock when, on hearing the sound of the front door opening, she tore herself away from the story of the family struggling to make ends meet in their crumbling, much-loved old castle. There had been times, she reflected, when her mother had struggled, but over these last few years, the business had been going from strength to strength.

Now, she sat, waiting for her to come through from the hallway, where, from the murmur of voices, she thought Diane was saying goodnight to her escort. Bonnie hoped she didn't need to meet Charlie Hamilton again until the morning, and still she felt curious as to why he'd been so deep in conversation with Patrik.

Her mother came into the room and closed the door gently behind her. She kicked off her high-heeled shoes and sank down on the sofa next to Bonnie.

"Did you enjoy yourself, Mum? Can I make you a bedtime drink?"

"It was a very pleasant evening, Bonnie. And, I don't need anything to drink, thanks. I've drunk two glasses of wine and that's more than enough for one night! How have you been getting on? Are all our guests in now?"

"They are. All's well, so I'll bolt the door now you and Mr Hamilton are back."

Her mum flexed her toes. "Thanks, love. It's ages since I did any ballroom dancing, but I think I managed not to tread on Charlie's feet, thank goodness. He might fancy himself as Fred Astaire, but I'm no Ginger Rogers!"

"But you got on well with him?"

"Yes, very well, thanks." She hesitated. "He talked about his time in the RAF during the war when he worked as ground staff. Told me he was still interested in aeroplanes and wished he'd learnt to fly one. He said he'd been proud to wear his uniform and enjoyed the discipline and comradeship during his service days.

"But, Bonnie, I still can't help wondering why he was so keen to know what the policemen said when they checked the honeymooners' room this morning. He certainly didn't hang around for long once he knew the cops were coming. Yet I can't understand, if he was so interested in that pair of rogues, why he didn't wait to see what the police made of it."

Bonnie longed to confide her niggling doubts in her mother, but knew she would only worry. Anyway, it was far too soon to tell her about Patrik. She kept her secret feelings close to her heart as she crossed the hallway to bolt the big door.

Her mother was still sitting on the sofa when Bonnie came back. "You must take some time off tomorrow, love. You've had a long day, and Kay's working tomorrow morning, so you could both go out after lunch and please yourselves for the rest of the day. How does that sound?"

"It sounds lovely, if you're sure, Mum?"

"Positive. Maybe you could go over to that café where they used to hold the tea dances back in the thirties and forties. You know, the old building that looks like a wedding cake?"

"It's called The Tivoli now. It used to be popular with fifth and sixth formers when I was at school." She paused. "It's where I met Tim."

Her mother pulled a face. "Oh dear, I'd forgotten that. Sorry, love. He turned out to be a big disappointment, I know."

"He didn't break my heart, Mum. And to be honest, I never ever felt about Tim, as I ..." She'd almost mentioned Patrik and heat flooded her cheeks as her mother stared at her.

"I meant to say, I never felt about Tim as I know Kay feels about Jack now." That was, Bonnie thought, perfectly true. Tim, having decided to join the Army, went about it without saying one word to Bonnie until the day before he left for training. In a way, it had been a relief and since then, she'd accepted invitations from several young men. Now she'd graduated from college and was working at home, the pool of eligible bachelors had dried up. Not that she cared about that too much.

Until now, maybe ...

The next morning sped by as normal, with its routine of tidying the dining room, making up beds and cleaning bathrooms. Charlie Hamilton slept in and turned up late for breakfast, but Bonnie took pity on him and made him scrambled eggs on toast which he ate while reading the

Sunday paper propped against a teapot. He left the guesthouse, cheerful as ever, around eleven thirty, delighted by Diane's offer of a roast dinner to be served at six o'clock that evening.

An old family friend who Bonnie had known as Uncle Sam when she was younger, and who owned his own building firm, had called round to see her mother and after chatting with Sam, she left the two of them together at the kitchen table, and went upstairs to change from her work outfit into a floral summer dress. She chose a dark red cotton frock, patterned with white daisies and put on a pair of open-toed white sandals. Daringly, she decided to go bare-legged, hoping her mum wouldn't notice. Even on very hot days, Diane was a stickler about wearing nylon stockings, especially on Sundays.

Kay had agreed with her they'd put their teenage years behind so wouldn't go out for coffee at the Tivoli, but grudgingly admitted there was no harm in visiting the pier once in a while. She'd gone home to change and the girls were to meet at the pier entrance at three o'clock. Kay's date with Jack wasn't until the evening, so she'd have plenty of time to nip home for tea before meeting him.

Bonnie left *Sea Breezes* too early for her meeting, but as if moving with a will of their own, her feet propelled her towards the funfair. After all, she'd promised Patrik she'd see him before too long. As she drew closer to the fairground, its familiar noises and smells drifted towards her on the breeze. If someone put her down, blindfolded, beside the entrance to the pleasure park, she would know precisely where she was.

As she walked past the children's roundabouts, she wondered if Patrik would be on duty. After all, he must have time off, though she knew, with such a brief holiday season, most employees worked all the hours they could, to save as much as possible before their jobs became summer memories. She felt a twinge of sadness for Patrik and his fellow-countrymen. It was probably even more difficult for them to find employment. He'd mentioned the career he'd been training for in Hungary, but being forced to flee his homeland, leaving behind precious possessions, made her wonder how he could continue his studies in his new country. She felt angry about the injustice of it.

The object of her thoughts was standing a few yards from the Waltzer, with his back to her. She called his name and, despite the usual loud music blaring over the loudspeakers, he turned to face her. For moments they gazed at one another, Bonnie feeling a whoosh of joy, as the slightly watchful expression on his face dissolved into a smile of pleasure.

"So good to see you, Bonnie." He reached out and took her right hand between both of his. "You are looking so beautiful. There is maybe some lucky young man waiting for you?"

Her heart flip-flopped, making her catch her breath. "Oh, no ... there's nobody, Patrik." *Except you*, she wanted to say. "I'm meeting Kay soon and after my work clothes, I fancied wearing a pretty dress."

His smile lit up his face. "I wish I had camera to take photograph of you."

Bonnie knew she was blushing. And he was still holding her hand. She looked across to the ride and noticed Patrik's boss inside the wooden booth. "Um, are you on a break?"

"Twenty minutes before I am due back."

She plucked up courage. "I'm meeting Kay at the pier. We could walk there together ... if you'd like to, of course."

"Really? Me in my overalls and you looking like a princess!" That gorgeous smile again ...

"Every princess needs a prince!" Bonnie couldn't believe she'd said that.

The expression on Patrik's face told her how much her comment meant to him. But did she really want to throw herself into a relationship that would probably lead nowhere, given his precarious situation? Once again, her emotions overcame any chance of logical thinking when she put her hand in his and felt him gently squeeze her fingers as he fell into step with her and they headed towards the funfair's exit.

Patrik wanted to know how many people were staying at the guesthouse. He didn't mention Charlie Hamilton and although Bonnie knew Patrik was aware that he was a regular guest, she didn't mention him either. Mr Hamilton had been in rather too much evidence over the last few days and unless Patrik spoke of him, she didn't intend bringing up the subject, though she had another matter on her mind.

"Have you seen anything of Jack?" Bonnie asked casually.

"A little."

She thought Patrik sounded guarded and wondered if he was aware of Jack's romantic adventures. It wouldn't do to question her new friend though. If Jack Williams really was up to no good, it was probably best if Bonnie didn't hear any of the gory details. Although, with her friend's interests at heart, she was still determined to tackle Jack if she bumped into him while she was on her own.

But Patrik glanced at her as they waited for a double-decker bus to trundle past before they crossed the road. "I do not know him well enough to talk about matters of the heart – if that is the proper expression – but I hope

Jack knows what he is doing."

He spoke the last part of his comment so fiercely, Bonnie flinched.

"I apologise," Patrik said softly when they'd reached the other pavement. "It is none of my concern."

"She's my oldest and best friend. I know someone made it their business to upset her, by telling her Jack was seeing another girl. Or, I could be mistaken and that person felt it right to tell Kay what was going on."

"Difficult for you. I know you all for such short time, but I don't like to think your friend has sadness because her boyfriend is ..."

"It's all right, Patrik, you don't need to say any more. I feel absolutely the same, as you can imagine. When Kay sees him this evening, I hope she asks him outright whether these rumours are true. All I can do is wait to see what happens and be there to pick up the pieces if necessary."

He squeezed her hand again. "You are perfect friend."

Bonnie chuckled. "We fall out sometimes. You know, squabble about silly things, but we stay friends."

"I like to be your friend, Bonnie. Already you become very important to me. I care about you."

The words she wanted to say in return wouldn't unscramble themselves in her brain. She and Patrik stopped walking. There was very little time remaining before he needed to return to his job. Why couldn't she say what she longed to say? How he was becoming important to her too? And, why couldn't she tell him to tread very carefully regarding Charlie Hamilton, when she possessed no proof that the man wasn't as straightforward in his business dealings as he might be?

All doubts and misgivings melted away as Patrik reached out a hand, gently brushing away a tendril of golden hair which the breeze had played with and left out of place. To her surprise, he drew her close. Kissed her on the lips. Kissed her so tenderly Bonnie almost burst into tears.

That brief kiss must have held a kind of magic. Because it dissolved all her doubts and misgivings over the rights and wrongs of becoming involved with Patrik. Her former boyfriend obviously hadn't cared enough about her and back then, her own feelings weren't deep enough to cause her real pain rather than hurt pride. Those fleeting romances which followed were with a medical student, a personnel manager and an earnest young man who worked in the dock offices and who'd frightened her away by suggesting they became engaged on only their third date.

All of these boyfriends came from the same kind of background as hers. Patrik came with a complicated back story. No prospects. No family in Great Britain apart from one brother. But those alarm bells which were ringing before were silenced now. Somehow, she must find a way to help him build a future in his new country. How she might achieve this still remained a mystery.

CHAPTER 10

Bonnie watched Patrik walk away. He turned around before crossing the road, to lift his hand in a farewell gesture. Left alone, Bonnie moved closer to the pier entrance and at once noticed two youths standing just inside the turnstile as if waiting for someone. She deliberately looked the other way, not wishing to make eye contact with either of them, and soon Kay arrived, looking like Sandra Dee in a pink and white gingham dress trimmed with broderie anglaise.

To her dismay, Bonnie couldn't help noticing bold stares coming their way from the two young men. The pair wore jeans and casual open-necked shirts and as she and her friend bought entrance tickets and walked past them, she decided they were probably day trippers and put them out of her mind. She was still floating on a fluffy pink cloud of joy and she was also relieved to find Kay in a much more positive mood after her heartfelt outburst the evening before.

"Well, did you go and see him?" Kay asked eagerly as the two strolled along the pier.

"Go and see who?"

Kay nudged Bonnie's elbow. "You know very well who! Come on, spill the beans."

"You sound," Bonnie said demurely, "like a character out of an Enid Blyton adventure story." She relented, seeing Kay's expression.

"Oh, all right then. Yes, I did see Patrik thank you. He had time to walk me over here before he went back to work."

"And?" Kay wouldn't let Bonnie off the hook.

"And we've arranged to meet on Tuesday evening. He gets a few hours off then as he's working tonight and all of tomorrow."

"Will you say anything to your mum?"

"Goodness, no, not yet!" Bonnie stopped walking. "Kay, promise me you won't say a single word? Not until I've told her myself."

"I knew it! You're serious about him, aren't you?"

"I think he's a very nice boy who's had a tough time. He never complains, even though some of his memories must be so sad ... so heart-breaking."

"Poor fellow. Compared to Jack who, in my opinion, has been very spoilt by his doting and misguided mum, Patrik is probably the more reliable of the two." She sighed.

Bonnie was sometimes surprised by her friend's perception. She couldn't help but agree with her, but decided it best not to say so.

"I hope things work out for you and Jack if that's what you really want, Kay. The boys who work at the funfair are bound to meet lots of girls. And the Wall of Death mechanics, let alone the stunt riders, attract more fans than the other rides do. People enjoy the thrill of it. If Jack has been seen talking to a girl, is that such a difficult thing to accept?"

"Of course not. Maybe I've been reading too much into the reason he was so keen to see me again after all this time. Getting too starry-eyed! It's probably best to see how this evening goes before I say something I might regret."

"Good thinking." Bonnie was impressed by her friend's logic and was about to say so when she felt a tap on the shoulder. She whirled around the instant Kay did the same. They were standing face to face with the two young men Bonnie had noticed eyeing them earlier.

"Good afternoon, girls. Fancy a bit of company?"

"No thanks," Kay said, quick as a flash. "We're meeting our boyfriends later."

Shoulder to shoulder, the pair moved forward, forcing the girls to step back to avoid being uncomfortably close to their unwelcome admirers. The skinnier of the two sniggered. "What if we don't believe you? Come on, girlies, we only want a bit of fun. How about we buy you both an ice cream, then take you on a nice gentle ride like the Tunnel of Love?"

"No, thank you," Bonnie said. "We're spoken for, so why don't you go and find someone else to keep you company, boys?"

The sturdier youth who hadn't yet made any comment, suddenly put his arm around her. At once she tried to break away but he wouldn't let go.

"Don't be so stuck up," he whispered in her ear, so she felt his hot breath.

She couldn't help shuddering, although she knew that would probably annoy him even more than her resistance. He was a lot taller than she was. And he was manoeuvring her slowly but surely towards a municipal hut which showed no signs of occupation.

"Leave her alone, you nincompoop!" Kay yelled.

"Shut your face!" The one who'd got hold of Kay hissed back as he gripped her arm. "The more you struggle, the keener we'll be! So be good little girlies and come and have a good time with us."

Bonnie looked around. She and Kay had walked a fair way down the pier, keeping to the side facing the quieter part of the bay. What if they started screaming for help? If there was a council employee in the hut, wouldn't he come out to see what was happening? She and Kay hadn't walked far enough for the anglers fishing from the end of the pier to hear them. They were in a kind of no man's land, trapped in a difficult situation with two men she despised for their bullying actions.

She could see Kay also looking around helplessly. This was horrible. Bonnie tried not to panic but to think quickly. If she and Kay pretended to change their minds and agree to accompany the hateful pair, that would take them back to the crowded promenade where Bonnie could pretend to be hit by sudden stomach pains and insist on going to the First Aid post. Kay would go with her and they could explain their predicament to the kindly St John's Ambulance team.

Bonnie took several deep breaths. Her attacker still held her in his grip. She relaxed a little but said nothing. Meanwhile, Kay was doing her best to kick and wriggle herself away from the other pest. She was screaming for help and sounded so distraught, she triggered Bonnie too, into yelling. Oh please! Surely someone would hear their screams and come to investigate?

Patrik felt as though a burden was lifted from his shoulders. The girl of his dreams had agreed to go out with him, though at that moment their date seemed a hundred years away. At once he thought of his appointment later that day and wondered if whatever Mr Hamilton had in mind would mean a little cash in hand. If so, he could take Bonnie to the ice cream parlour or even to the smart café called the Tivoli and in which he'd never set foot.

Only moments ago, he'd felt like running across the beach and splashing through the shallows. Kicking up the frothing sea water and laughing for sheer joy! Now, for some strange reason he felt tense. And this had nothing to do with his appointment later. Patrik hadn't felt totally comfortable since looking back at Bonnie and noticing those two youths hanging around at the entrance to the pier. He could of course be mistaken and they were only waiting for someone to turn up.

But the way they studied Bonnie had made his flesh crawl. Made him ball his fists at the side of his body as he walked away. An involuntary reaction which had happened many times while he was still in Hungary. Fortunately, this had been a rare occurrence since his arrival in South Wales, but even so, he trusted his instincts and despite the risk of being late for work, Patrik knew he must turn back and check Kay had turned up to meet her friend and that the young men had drifted off.

He felt in his pocket for change, suddenly anxious he mightn't have enough money on him to cover his entrance fee for the pier. If he explained to the ticket seller, would they understand his fears? Would they allow him to check? He dreaded them hearing his foreign accent and seeing that look of suspicion which he encountered now and then. Phew! He huffed air through his lips as he took out enough coins to cover the entrance fee.

Maybe he was being silly? There was no sign of either Bonnie or Kay, nor of the two youths. He hoped they'd gone in different directions. Hoped he was wrong to worry. Yet, Patrik couldn't change his mind having come this far. He'd walk down the pier as quickly as he could while scanning faces on the way. Two pretty girls, one with curly blonde hair and the other with an auburn ponytail, shouldn't prove difficult to spot. There was still no sign of the two youths and he had no way of knowing whether they'd just bought their tickets or were about to leave the pier. As long as they hadn't followed the two girls, Patrik could turn around and hurry back to complete his shift before making ready for his evening appointment.

Trying to conceal his impatience, he fell in line behind a young family, the husband counting out coins for two adults and three children, while Patrik waited his turn.

"One ticket please." He pushed the right money beneath the glass screen separating the ticket seller from the customers.

The instant the attendant pushed Patrik's ticket towards him, he grabbed it, called out a polite thank you and pushed through the turnstile. This was his first visit to the pier and he found himself looking down at the wooden planks, the waves lapping below clearly visible through narrow gaps between the boards.

Which side to take? There were shelters, some with people sitting in them, at intervals along the boardwalk. Here and there were kiosks selling ice creams or candy floss and sticks of peppermint rock. He spotted a little coffee bar and paused to look inside as he continued walking down the right-hand side. He upped his pace a little. It wasn't too crowded. He could continue to the end, then walk back up the other side towards the exit.

Still no sign of the girls. He would be reassured to see those two youths whether on their own or with other people apart from Bonnie and Kay, so he kept on searching, his eyes darting here, there and everywhere. Until, further along, his heart thumping and bumping in his chest, he stopped in his tracks, straining to hear what he knew at once wasn't the plaintive squawk of a hungry seagull. Where had the sound come from? Patrik hurried on but saw nothing. He could no longer hear anything. Doubling back, he stopped to listen. Realisation dawned.

Patrik slipped through the gap between a shelter and a small hut which certainly wasn't selling rock or candy floss. But if a custodian used it, there was no sign of anyone being around. And, as he reached the other side, there they were! Bonnie and Kay, each one being restrained by one of the two youths he'd been searching for. The girls were struggling to get away. Patrik took a deep breath.

He sprang forward. For whatever reason, the first word that left his lips was 'Desist!' Patrick wasn't a man of violence, but his fury drove him on and with a roar, he grabbed the first youth and wrenched him away from Kay, sending him staggering.

"Patrik," she cried. "Oh, thank goodness you're here."

"Stupid girls." Bonnie's assailant had let go of her as if she was on fire. He winked at Patrik. "No need for you to worry, mate. You know what birds are like. Always leading a bloke on."

Patrik lunged and pinned both the second youth's arms behind him. "I am not your mate and you are lucky I do not report you to the police for assault!"

Bonnie and Kay were clinging to one another though fortunately didn't appear to have been injured.

"Should I ask pier attendant to dial 999?" Patrik asked.

"Hey, are you one of them refugees? Who are you to throw your weight about?"

The girls exchanged looks. "These two need to be taught a lesson," Kay said. "They're a pair of stupid jerks who deserve a night in the cells for treating us like they did."

"I agree." Bonnie addressed the two culprits who

stood, sullen-faced, in front of the pier rail, while Patrik stood, glowering at them. Daring them to make one false move.

"We'd like an apology," Bonnie said. "And we want you to go straight back where you came from, but not until you put money in the St John's Ambulance collection box."

"Or, give the money to us and we'll make sure it goes in," Kay added. "Otherwise, my friend and I will run down the pier, screaming our heads off until we find an official who we can report you to. Patrik here will be our eye witness. Despite your stupid comment, he's a hardworking member of the community."

Both Bonnie and Patrik gazed at her in admiration.

The skinnier youth shook his head but reached inside his jacket and took out his wallet.

Kay held out her hand. "And don't forget we expect an apology as well."

The other youth made as if to move sideways and escape while Patrik kept an eye on what his mate was up to, but Bonnie was too quick for him.

"You won't out-run Patrik. And if you even think about it, we'll make a formal complaint. Believe me, that'll mean a long, uncomfortable night cooling your heels in a police cell."

Once apologies had been given and at least ten shillings handed over to Kay, Patrik and the girls escorted the sulky pair to the turnstile. Patrik gave them one more whispered warning and though the girls couldn't quite make out what he was saying, it was evident the words were hitting home.

Watching the pair drift off, heads down, towards the railway station, Bonnie turned to their rescuer. "We can't thank you enough. But what made you come on the pier when I thought you were going straight back to the

Waltzer?"

He placed his right hand on his heart. "I have bad feeling when I saw those fellows keeping their eyes on you. I set off for work, but something made me turn around to make sure you were OK."

"Gosh," Kay exclaimed as she watched Bonnie fly into his arms. "This is even better than going to see *Tammy and the Bachelor* at the cinema last week!"

CHAPTER 11

"He was so brave," Kay said as the girls watched Patrik sprinting towards the pleasure park. "By the way, your cheeks are pink and your eyes all sparkly." She grinned mischievously. "I can't say I'm surprised!"

Bonnie smiled. "I still can't believe how he came to find us."

"I can't wait to tell Jack. And you must say something to your mum, now. You really must."

They were almost at the First Aid station on the promenade. Kay was clutching the money ready to donate. "She's bound to be impressed when you tell her how brave your young man was."

Bonnie waited as her friend handed over the cash and received a big thank you from the team on duty. There seemed no point in explaining the story behind it.

"Shall we go to that little café on the way to your house?" she suggested. "You won't be too far away to go back for your tea then."

"Good idea. I think we deserve a treat after all that. Those two have made me want to take up boxing!"

Bonnie chuckled. "Are girls allowed to do that, I wonder?"

Kay wrinkled her nose. "I doubt it. But I hated feeling so helpless back there. In broad daylight with people around and you and I still managed to find trouble."

"More like trouble found us, wasn't it? I could kick myself for not telling you those two were hanging around when I arrived. They were actually inside the turnstile so if we'd gone through just a few minutes later, I bet they'd have been off looking for some other poor girls to pester. I'm sorry, Kay."

"I can't help thinking it was good they got their comeuppance from Patrik. But we mustn't let what happened spoil the rest of our day."

"I hope all goes well between you and Jack. I'll probably watch the TV with Mum."

"And dream about your knight in shining armour? So, will you tell Diane about him now? Go on, I dare you!"

They reached the café and sat down at an outside table. Bonnie ordered two strawberry milkshakes, both with a scoop of vanilla ice cream. "It's early days. We hardly know each other and you know how over-protective my mum can be, even though I'm nineteen. She was married with me on the way at the same age."

"Doesn't that mean she should be sympathetic about you falling for someone lovely like Patrik?"

Bonnie sighed and fiddled with the long silver spoon the waitress had placed before her. "In one way, yes, but what if she has a problem with him being Hungarian? He belongs to a totally different culture."

"Yes, but does that matter? You told me your dad sailed all around the world when he was in the Merchant Navy. He must have mixed with all kinds of nationalities, surely? We went to school with Greek girls and Jewish girls. And when you used to invite me along to those students' union hops, didn't we dance with boys from Africa and the Caribbean, over here to study?"

"Of course." Bonnie waited while the milkshakes

arrived and the waitress sped off again. "Then I met Tom ..."

"And he had about as much personality as a face flannel."

Bonnie burst out laughing. "Well, he did me a favour when he dropped me like a slippery bar of soap, don't you think?"

"Definitely. Goodness, this milkshake is lush, but heaven help me if I can't eat whatever my mother has cooked for tea!" Kay waved her spoon in the air. "Obviously, it's up to you whether you say anything to your mum or not, but I think it's a crying shame you can't boast about Patrik's bravery."

Patrik worked the rest of his shift, relieved to have no time to think. He was much faster now, when giving change to the customers and his English, according not only to Bonnie, but also to his boss, was improving day by day. He spoke in his own language while with his friends in the caravan and he would never give up using his mother-tongue, but realised the importance of speaking good English.

The caravan's facilities were very basic but he made sure to have a proper wash, razored off his dark stubble and put on his only decent pair of trousers with a white shirt and jacket. He'd borrowed a pair of shoes from his brother but as he'd no idea what the evening might bring, workwise, he rolled up a clean pair of dungarees and sat down on his bunk to read a Sunday paper discarded by one of the riders. Patrik's honest nature had prompted him to keep the newspaper in the kiosk in case its owner returned to claim it, but his boss was happy for him to take it when his shift ended. He was pleased to have another opportunity to learn more new words.

He tried his best to read an article telling how, on the 12th July 1957, twenty-year-old Prince Karim had become Aga Khan on the death of his grandfather. The young prince was studying at Harvard University, somewhere Patrik had heard of, but he stumbled over a few of the words though he had a feeling these referred to subjects like religion and spirituality and weren't everyday words that he used much more easily now.

A short horn blast startled him. He jumped to his feet, dropping the newspaper onto his bunk, then headed straight out of the caravan, collecting his rolled-up dungarees on the way. No one ever bothered to lock the door. Who would want to steal any of the young men's meagre belongings? Charlie Hamilton was at the wheel of a shiny red car, engine ticking over, and he leaned across to open the passenger door.

"Thank you." Patrik got in.

"Bang on time, well done." Charlie switched on the car's sidelights and put the car in gear. "I see you've brought work clothes."

"I forgot to check with you if I needed them."

"Probably not, but I like the way you've come prepared. Good thinking."

Streaks of peach, rust and terracotta painted the sky in a fiery sunset that evening. Patrik looked out of the window at the peaceful old harbour on his left. "It is pretty coastline, all along here. I like the golden sands and I like the pebbled beaches."

"Did your family live on the coast? If Hungary actually does have a coast – my geography's a bit shaky."

"We are a landlocked country. I think that is correct word. But there are lakes and River Danube runs through the middle."

Charlie nodded. "And where's your home?"

Patrik swallowed hard, fighting a sudden surge of homesickness. "My parents had a house not far from Budapest." He saw a vision of the four-bedroomed stone dwelling flash into his mind's eye.

"Ah, now that I have heard of!"

Patrik couldn't find the words to express the sights and sounds he'd experienced what now seemed years ago, although were still so vivid in his memory that they might have happened only hours before. He thought Charlie was showing an interest in him probably to put him at ease, but Patrik preferred not to discuss his recent painful past.

"Sometimes it is best to leave the past behind and concentrate on the future," he said after a while.

"You're not wrong about that," Charlie said. They were driving up a steep hill lined with houses either side. This was a part of the town Patrik didn't know but he gazed at the different styles property while the car took the gradient, until its driver took a left turn and the number of houses dwindled until all he could see were fields and farmhouses.

"This is the road to Faircliff Airport," Charlie said. "It's only a few miles from the town. I'm going to introduce you to Ken, the chap who looks after my business affairs at this end. Import and export, you know."

Patrik didn't know. He'd no idea what import actually meant as it was another new word. "Sorry, but new word for me, Charlie. This is about flying, I think?"

"Goods being flown in, yes. Items being flown into the country by suppliers in foreign places. That's really all you need to know, mate. Ken will explain everything as we go along."

Patrik wondered exactly where they'd be going along but decided to say nothing. Sometimes the English language could be very mysterious. As for the Welsh language ... he was thankful when Bonnie told him hardly anyone in the town spoke it after leaving school. At least that was a complication he could avoid, though he sympathised with people who loved their mother tongue and hoped plenty of folk spoke Welsh at home.

Before long, he noticed the outlines of what looked like a control tower in the middle of a cluster of low buildings, and beyond them to the left, the unmistakeable silhouette of a large hangar. Charlie flicked on his right-hand indicator, but instead of driving onto the deserted forecourt adjoining the main building, he drove on to a track which Patrik soon realised led to the hangar.

Charlie pulled up around the side furthest from the terminal and office buildings. At once, a man dressed in dark clothing, appeared from a door Patrik hadn't noticed and walked towards them.

"Don't get out for the moment, son," Charlie said, opening the driver's door.

Patrik said nothing. There seemed to be no one around, apart from the three of them so he decided Sunday flights must all be over. But this was a small airport. He'd never flown though he'd seen newsreels at the cinema back in Budapest and marvelled at the different aeroplanes and the passengers who could afford to fly in them.

Charlie tapped on his window before opening the passenger door. "Come and meet Ken. He'll explain what duties you'll be carrying out, so listen carefully and if you don't understand, ask Ken. I'd like you to start working for me as soon as possible."

"I ... I hadn't properly decided yet, sir – I mean Charlie – about taking the job on."

There wasn't a great deal of daylight left but Patrik

could still see how Charlie Hamilton's lips met in a thin line.

"That, Patrik, is my decision. I think you have what it takes but I can't stand ditherers."

Patrik wanted to ask what a ditherer was but realised he must do as he was told and hope for the best.

"You can use some extra money, can't you? You didn't have a win on the football pools last night, I take it?"

"No, I di ...did not," Patrik stammered.

"Then follow Ken and take note while I check on a few details." He walked ahead of the other two and entered the hangar.

"He likes to take a look around the old crate now and then," Ken said. "Never really adapted to civilian life in my humble opinion. Has he told you about his wartime exploits yet?"

CHAPTER 12

Once home again, Bonnie wandered into the garden where her mother was tidying up flowerbeds.

"I'm back, Mum, if you want to go out."

"I think I'll do a bit more out here, Bonnie, but a cup of tea wouldn't go amiss if you're in the mood. All our guests are out, just so's you know."

"I had a giant milkshake with Kay, but I'll make you a cuppa." Bonnie headed off to prepare a tray.

There was a contraption which clanged outside when someone rang the front door bell so callers weren't left hanging about in the porch. While she set out tea things, Bonnie thought how much her feelings had changed towards Patrik in such a short time. Even though she knew so little about his life in Hungary, she felt at ease with him though still excited and, if she was honest, a tiny bit worried about her mum's reaction to this romance. For it was a romance – Bonnie was certain of that now.

"Time to take a break!" Bonnie called as she carried the tray outside. She placed it on the wrought iron table in front of the garden bench. There were a couple of folding chairs out there too, in case any of the guests fancied a little tranquillity, but usually visitors were keen to make the most of the seaside activities.

Diane Morgan put down her ancient shears and did

as her daughter asked. "Now, before we go any further, I know something's up, but if my maternal instincts are correct, it's nothing to worry about. In fact, I'm pretty sure you're hugging a rather special secret to yourself." She sat down on the cushioned seat. "Ah, that's better..."

Startled, Bonnie sat down beside her. She had a fair idea what this was all about, but waited to hear what else her mother had to say.

"You're wondering what I'm going to say next ..." Her mum stirred the pot and sat back.

"I might've known you'd guess something had happened." Bonnie spoke softly as she fixed her gaze on her mum's favourite tea roses.

"Sweetheart, you don't have to tell me anything, but if you ever want to talk ..."

Even at nineteen years of age, Bonnie felt the urge to snuggle closer to Diane. "The thing is, Mum, I've met someone, but it's early days so I decided not to say anything yet."

"I know that feeling."

Bonnie reached out to pour the tea. Her mother's remark sounded so heartfelt, but surely, she couldn't be referring to Bonnie's late father?

"When I first met your dad, I was afraid to say anything to my parents," Diane said.

"Gosh, why was that?"

"Because he'd already joined the Merchant Navy and I knew your grandmother in particular wouldn't approve. They had their sights set on me marrying a young man who lived two doors down from us and who worked in a bank. Steady hours, good prospects and all that."

"Did you go out with him?" Bonnie, fascinated now, hadn't heard this before.

"Only once, and not long before I met your father at a tea dance. I'd gone along with another girl and George was also there with a friend."

"And that was it? You knew he was the one?"

"Both of us felt the same, but our first date was a foursome with the other couple, though they didn't hit it off, whereas George and I got on well, right from the start. Only a week or so later he told me he'd decided we were meant for each other, the moment he clapped eyes on me at the dance." She gazed at the same rose bush but Bonnie knew her mother was picturing something, or maybe somebody else in her mind's eye.

"You've never said much before. It's really bittersweet, Mum."

"My parents' generation didn't believe in showing their emotions. It's hard to shake off that kind of attitude when you've been brought up to do the same, but you're a grown woman now and a beautiful one at that. Some young fellow's bound to fall in love with you and you with him. I never thought Tim was right for you, by the way."

Bonnie shook her head slowly. "You kept that under your hat, didn't you?"

"Of course. I knew there was no danger of you deciding to marry him. I only met him a couple of times, but it struck me that a doughnut had more personality than that young man!"

Bonnie burst out laughing. "I must tell Kay. She said the same, but in her case, she suggested a face flannel."

Diane Morgan chuckled. "Good for Kay. It didn't surprise me when Tim vanished from your life, but the last thing a daughter needs to hear is her mother saying 'I told you so!'

They sat in silence for a while. Next door's black cat slunk through the shrubbery and, as if he had all the time in the world, prowled down the path only to turn around and take his usual route through a hole in the fence as soon as he noticed them.

This seemed to prompt Bonnie's mother to make a comment. "You have time on your side, love. I was born at the end of the Great War, during which as you know, many young men lost their lives. Your father was five years older than me and he didn't get called up until the second world war was underway. You, of course, were born the year before it began. In a way, I must have seen more of George than most wives saw their husbands, because at that time, he was returning to his home port and staying a few days before setting off again."

"I wish I could've got to know him better." Bonnie spoke quietly. "There are so many little memories, but it's rather like having a jigsaw puzzle that you can't finish."

Her mum said nothing for a few moments but squeezed Bonnie's hand. "He was always so proud of you, love. Never forget that."

Unthinkingly, Bonnie blurted out something she hadn't meant to say. "I wonder what he'd have thought of Patrik!"

She woke at around six next morning, having found it difficult to fall asleep until well after midnight. Thoughts had been milling around in her head and try as she might, she'd been unable to calm them. Her mother, on hearing Patrik's name, asked how she'd met him and Bonnie explained, also saying he was twenty-one years old. Diane didn't press for information but Bonnie knew her mother would be questioning the credentials of a young man who'd taken a summer job bound to end in September. She longed to explain Patrik's predicament but decided it best to say no more for the present.

Before sleep claimed her, Bonnie had lain awake, pondering over spotting Patrik talking to Charlie Hamilton and, inevitably, she began fretting over some unknown possibly which was completely beyond her control. There were always people ready to take advantage of others more vulnerable and though Patrik was intelligent, young and healthy, red question marks surrounded not only his future, but his current job plus his accommodation.

As soon as Bonnie got downstairs, her mother asked her to take Mr Hamilton his early morning tea tray. There was nothing she could do except carry out the task. She knew Kay would arrive soon, but if she asked her friend to swap duties, Kay would immediately wonder why. She'd jump to conclusions and maybe suspect Charlie of making a pass at Bonnie, the idea of which horrified her. There was nothing creepy about Charlie, and his behaviour was always gentlemanly and respectful. So, why did she feel suspicious? What was it about her mother's most regular guest that concerned her?

Bonnie tapped at Charlie's door and immediately heard him call, "Come in."

Well-trained by her mother, she bid him "Good Morning" and kept her tray steady while heading for the bedside table, even though she realised Charlie, wearing a maroon dressing gown, was sitting in the easy chair beside the window.

"Lovely morning again, Bonnie. I like it when the sun wakes me."

"It's beautiful, Mr Hamilton. I should've got up when I woke, and gone for a dip."

"I swim like a stone, but I can appreciate how much you value living on the coast."

It was, she felt, as if each of them was well aware the other might be on their guard. She didn't know this man well, but he'd been walking in and out of her life for several years now and he'd known her since the days she'd worn a wire brace to straighten her front teeth. He'd teased her about the lime green socks she'd worn the year she became a teenager and he'd bought her a box of chocolates on her sixteenth birthday when he happened to be staying. She knew her mother thought the world of him, though the two weren't romantically involved, but Bonnie's unwelcome suspicions wouldn't go away.

Early that afternoon, when Diane left to catch a bus into town, Kay and Bonnie made themselves a sandwich.

"Shall we take our lunch into the garden?" Bonnie suggested.

"Why not? As long as I keep out of the sun. I don't want any more freckles."

"OK, you take the plates and I'll make up some orange squash."

In the garden, washing flapped on the line, hung out as always, with the hope that no seagulls flying overhead would dare spoil its pristine condition.

"We can have a good catch-up," Kay said as she sank down on the bench.

"Well, you're the one with the most going on at the moment," Bonne said. "I can't wait to hear whether you had it out with Jack."

"Um ... well, not really. He was quieter than usual and somehow, I couldn't bring myself to wheedle anything out of him."

"I can understand that, but I don't like to think of you being two-timed, especially as he was so quick to ask you to go out with him. If he really is seeing someone else, it's not fair on you or the other girl."

Kay stared down at her sandwich. "I enjoyed the film and he held my hand through most of it. Then when he walked me home, he hugged me and gave me a goodnight kiss, but I won't tell you what he whispered in my ear because I'm afraid I might jinx the pair of us!"

"OK. By the look on your face, I can imagine exactly what he said." Bonnie told herself Jack couldn't possibly be so cruel as to let down her friend. Not when she guessed he'd uttered those three little words which she knew Kay had longed to hear. Probably she'd been more upset than she let on, when Jack finished with her that first time.

"We're not going to see one another for a few days now. That was my suggestion, by the way." Kay bit into her sandwich.

"What did he say to that?"

Kay pointed to her mouth and went on chewing. Bonnie decided to start eating too, picturing the pile of ironing lurking in the scullery.

"Well, he seemed disappointed," Kay said at last. "He asked me if it was something he'd said or done, so I told him it was nothing of the sort. I told him I needed a few days to sort out my feelings."

"Gosh, good for you. If you don't mind my saying so, that was a very mature decision."

"Thank you. Now how about you? It's tomorrow night you have your date with Patrik, isn't it?"

Bonnie swallowed, feeling that floating on a fluffy pink cloud sensation. "Yes. I'm not sure what we're doing yet, but he's going to walk up the hill and wait for me on the corner."

"He's very protective of you. I was thinking that after he came to our rescue yesterday. You're a lucky girl."

"I know, but don't you think Jack would've done the same, had he been in Patrik's place?"

"I like to think so." Kay reached for her glass. "Now tell me what you're planning to wear for your date. And shall I give you a manicure after we finish work tomorrow?"

Bonnie wailed. "I don't know! What I do know is Patrik doesn't have many clothes because he had to leave so much behind in Hungary and he's short of money, so I daren't dress up and wear make-up in case he feels bad about not taking me out for a meal and that'd make both of us feel terrible then." She huffed a deep breath.

"Patrik wouldn't have asked you out if all he had to wear was his work clothes. And I'm not suggesting you dress up to the nines. If I put your hair up for you and give your nails a couple of coats of pale pink polish, you'll feel well-groomed without looking as if you're all dolled up with nowhere to go. Deal?"

CHAPTER 13

Next day, Patrik was panicking. He'd managed to borrow a shirt and rousers that were smarter than the only ones he possessed. Once again, he'd borrowed a pair of shoes to wear on his date with Bonnie. Istvan had joked with him, teasing him about being a ladies' man, though Patrik knew his big brother was pleased for him.

But when he returned to his caravan on completing his shift, he found an envelope bearing his name, pushed beneath the door. Inside was a note from Charlie Hamilton, instructing him to be ready to be collected that evening at half past seven. Patrik was devastated, having arranged to meet Bonnie at seven that evening. He was sure Charlie had told him he wouldn't be needed until later in the week.

He needed to act quickly. If he let his new boss down, that would put paid to any further work. If he stood Bonnie up ... here he imagined his heart almost stopped beating as dismay consumed him. This lovely girl lit up his life. Her positive attitude gave him hope for the future. He couldn't and mustn't let her down. But what if he could speak to her in time and confide his dilemma? It had to be worth a try. He needed to act fast.

Some kind soul had donated a second-hand bicycle to the lads living in the caravan. Patrik was still in his work clothes – still had time to stop Bonnie from wondering whether he'd forgotten about their date. Although his heart told him he was crazy, his head overruled his emotions and he knew, if he could only explain his dilemma, Bonnie would understand his desire to improve his prospects. Patrik left the caravan, grabbed the clapped-out bicycle and set off, pedalling furiously, towards *Sea Breezes*.

He wore no wrist watch. Both he and his companions depended on the alarm clock in the caravan. At the Waltzer, his boss informed him when it was time to take a break, go for lunch or finish his shift. He knew there was time to spare before Bonnie was ready, though he felt the sooner he could speak to her, the better it would be. When the slope up to her road made it impossible for him to keep pedalling, he dismounted and walked as fast as possible, pushing the cycle, then parking it neatly outside the house before sprinting up to the porch. He barely took in his surroundings but what he saw reminded him very poignantly of his former family home. Patrik pushed away the painful thought.

He rang the doorbell and heard it chime. Soon he heard the sound of someone calling before the door swung open.

"Patrik! Have you got the time wrong?" Kay stood there. "Bonnie's nowhere near ready."

He could see her eyeing his dungarees and probably wondering what he was playing at. "So sorry, but I need to speak with her about ... about our appointment together. I have a problem and it's important she knows this is difficulty for me."

"Don't worry – I'll tell her you're here, but you mustn't stand outside. Come in and wait."

"Thank you. I don't wish to be of any trouble to Mrs Morgan." He stepped over the threshold and instantly felt at home. That smell of furniture polish and the scent drifting from a vase of roses ... there was a good feel to this house. Once again, he felt nostalgic, remembering his own home, also the holidays in his grandparents' country house. Patrik, who relied a lot upon his own judgement, wished he felt equally positive about his future role in Charlie Hamilton's 'other' business. So far, nobody knew Patrik had been approached – not even his brother Istvan. He'd obeyed instructions.

Kay came back. "She'll be with you in a minute."

"Thank you."

He watched her disappear down the corridor then turned as he heard someone hurrying downstairs. Seeing Bonnie dressed in a floral housecoat and with nothing on her feet, he could feel his cheeks heat. And he couldn't stop his eyes from widening at sight of her golden locks, upswept and away from her oval face. The colour of her eyes reminded him of the vivid blue flowers growing in the cornfields he'd seen as a child, when visiting his grandparents.

Now totally lost for words, he realised she was waiting for him to say something. He stood to attention and gave her a little bow.

"Goodness, Patrik, has something happened? I hope you haven't received bad news."

"No! Well, bad in one very big way, but not bad in another, I guess." He managed a smile.

"You're here to tell me you can't see me tonight. Is that it?"

"It is the reason why I come, yes." He saw the disappointment in her expression and wanted to put his arms around her, but that didn't seem the correct thing to do when she wasn't properly dressed. "I have last minute request to help someone out this evening. I would not wish to change plans for you and me, Bonnie, but I hope you will understand I have good reason to do such thing."

"You've come here specially to tell me. I ... I've been looking forward to spending time with you, Patrik, but if things are difficult for you, then of course you must do what's most urgent."

He hated hearing her sound so disappointed. How could he do this to her? "Believe me, Bonnie, I much prefer to be with you this evening, but Mister ..."

He'd almost let slip Charlie's name and he knew Bonnie could see his discomfort. Patrik watched her expression change. Holding his breath. Wondering what she might be thinking.

"Patrik, please forgive me for asking, but does whatever this is all about, have anything to do with Mr Hamilton? I mean Charlie Hamilton, the man who stays with us."

He looked at his feet. This was dreadful. He was sworn to silence. Yet the girl of his dreams was wondering what could be more important to him than their planned evening out. But why did she suspect Charlie was involved? Did Bonnie know something Patrik should be aware of?

Anxious thoughts nagged at him while he tried to decide how best to deal with Bonnie's question. And to add further difficulty to his situation, a lady was coming downstairs and even from one swift glance, he recognised her as an older version of Bonnie. And here he was, wearing his sturdy dungarees, and wishing things could be different. Would he ever turn his life around and convince Bonnie of his deep feelings for her?

"Bonnie?" Diane walked towards them. "Is everything all right? Can I help?"

"Mum, it's fine. I'll come through in a minute. OK?"

Patrik did his best to look calm. Almost on auto-pilot he gave Bonnie's mother another of his little bows then smiled at her.

She smiled back. "Bonnie? Aren't you going to introduce us? I imagine this young man's not enquiring about accommodation."

"Oh, sorry, Mum. This is Patrik Matyaz. Patrik this is my mother, Diane Morgan."

He stepped forward to shake her hand. "I'm pleased to meet the mother of my good friend, Bonnie."

"Well, it's nice to meet you too, Patrik. I'll leave you to it then."

Bonnie waited for her mother to close the kitchen door before surprising Patrik by taking both his hands in hers. "We need to talk. But this isn't the right time or place. When can we meet?"

Patrik left *Sea Breezes* feeling disgruntled though he didn't know the English word for his feelings. He hadn't liked seeing Bonnie look anxious when she guessed he was involved with Charlie Hamilton, nor had he enjoyed postponing his date with her. She'd suggested she came down to the pleasure park next day and wait in the café where they'd gone that night with Kay and Jack, until Patrik could join her for his break. They wouldn't have long together, but at least they could clear the air, or so he hoped. By then of course he'd have carried out whatever Charlie had in mind for him that evening. Bonnie had promised to share her concerns with him and his feelings for her were too strong for him to risk upsetting her by not keeping his side of the bargain.

Then of course he risked Charlie's displeasure, should he learn Patrik had told Bonnie about his 'moonlighting' which he knew was an English word to describe someone who took a second job, usually a job involving night working. Patrik still couldn't understand why such a thing should remain a secret. This was

Wales, not Hungary.

He cycled back to the caravan, free-wheeling down the hill but taking care not to whizz along too quickly. He should have ample time left before Charlie's driver collected him in a black Morris Minor motor car. He'd been advised to wear old clothes, something which, Patrik thought ruefully, wasn't a problem for him.

He washed his face and brushed his hair, then opened the caravan door so he could keep watch for the black car. He didn't have long to wait.

Bonnie and Kay were standing in the porch. Kay was about to go home.

"It's such a shame! I was going to suggest we went to the pictures, but it's a bit late now."

"I'm sorry you've taken the trouble to do my hair and nails and all for nothing. Though," Bonnie added, "at least Patrik saw my new hairdo."

"He looked so upset, poor chap. It was obvious he hated having to call things off."

"Yes, well I'll see him tomorrow and make sure there's nothing too awful going on."

"Do you mean like bad news from his brother? Do they still have family in Hungary, I wonder?"

"I honestly don't know. I hope it's nothing too dreadful. I imagine he and Istvan have seen enough awful things to last them a lifetime."

"Your mum's bound to question you. Are you sure you don't want me to stay?"

Bonnie shook her head. "It's a very kind offer, Kay, but Mum already knew about Patrik. I accidentally let slip his name. It's just that I wouldn't normally expect to introduce a new boyfriend to my mother after knowing him such a short time."

"He's not got himself in some kind of trouble, has

he? You know you can trust me not to say anything. Not that anyone else knows him apart from Jack."

Bonnie shrugged. "Except, the other day, when I was walking through the funfair, I happened to see Patrik talking to Mr Hamilton."

Kay frowned. "I didn't know they knew one another."

"Mr Hamilton offered to come looking for me the night of the fire. Patrik walked me back home, remember? They met then, but only for moments." She knew she mustn't say more than that.

"Maybe Mr Hamilton was just passing the time of day with Patrik. He always seems interested in what's going on. I get the impression he thinks of your mum and you as family."

"I'm sure you're right, Kay. It's good that he remembered Patrik."

But as Bonnie went back into the house, she still felt anxious. The conversation she'd seen on the pleasure park looked far more significant than it would have, if the two men were simply being sociable. But Bonnie didn't want Kay knowing that. Not until she'd reassured herself by speaking to Patrik

"Here we go." Ken, who made sure to introduce himself again to Patrik as Charlie's right-hand man, opened the driver's door. "Just follow me. Do as I say and don't speak unless you're spoken to."

They'd arrived at the dockyard where Ken had parked beside a big warehouse. Patrik got out of the car and walked in silence beside the other man. He cast uneasy glances to his right, where the bulky shapes of craft moored alongside the dock loomed in the semi-darkness. To his left, unprotected by any barrier, lay a narrow channel of water, lapping against the stone sides of the culvert. Patrik shivered at the thought of tumbling into its dangerous depths. Falling into the main dock would be bad enough, but the prospect of plunging into these sinister waters so close to him was nightmarish. Back in Hungary he'd had to swim across rivers while making his bid for freedom – a far more hazardous occupation than swimming off a golden, sandy beach while holidaying back in the days when life seemed to be filled with opportunities.

Patrik told himself to stop obsessing about unpleasant experiences. They were nearing a shed at the end of the wharf and he jumped as Ken nudged his right elbow and muttered an instruction.

"When I hand you the cartons one by one, let me know when you can't carry any more."

Patrik stood aside as the older man gave four separate taps on the door. It seemed an age before anyone responded and when they did, he saw a man dressed in overalls and wearing a black balaclava mask. He and Ken exchanged a few words then Ken beckoned to Patrik to follow them.

The shed was lit by a bare bulb hanging from a rafter. The dank, dreary interior with its shadowy corners made Patrik think of rats lurking in outhouses and barns where he'd taken refuge with his companions while journeying towards the next border. He wasn't a coward, but his survival instinct remained sharpened by past events and now he wondered exactly what he'd let himself in for. Silently he prayed there were no drugs involved in this secret venture. That he could not possibly tolerate. Not for the first time, he wished he'd never agreed to becoming involved.

The men ahead of him had stopped walking. Patrik guessed this meant the one in the balaclava was pointing out which cartons were to be taken away.

"We start here, Patrik," Ken said. "Hold your arms out in front of you."

Patrik obeyed. One carton wasn't very heavy but five was his limit although one more than his overseer was able to carry. The two made several trips from the shed back to the vehicle, after which Ken exchanged whispered words with the man who'd allowed them access to the stocks while Patrik got back into the car to wait.

Patrik's chauffeur didn't hang around long. He got back behind the wheel and turned the car round without saying a word. Patrik itched to question him about the goods they were transporting but decided it best to hold his tongue. He didn't want Charlie Hamilton thinking Patrik was too nosey for his own good. Yet, without knowing exactly what he'd become involved with, how could he sleep easy at night?

CHAPTER 14

At *Sea Breezes*, they were halfway through yet another week. During the peak holiday season, Diane could rarely offer accommodation for only a night or two until she tore off the calendar page for August. She and the girls measured their summer in weekly segments. After a few nights, couples were usually chatting with other couples in the dining room, or when they met in the residents' lounge. That midweek morning, Bonnie paid special attention to Charlie, whose custom was much-valued, and who was the only guest staying on his own. He appeared calm and cheerful as usual. It was hard to understand his odd behaviour the weekend before, when he discovered Diane was anticipating another police visit. Bonnie still wondered what reason he had for what appeared to be a fit of the jitters.

She was serving him his usual cooked breakfast when she heard the telephone ring. There was an extension in the kitchen and she knew Kay would answer the call if her mother was busy. Charlie was asking her whether she'd seen *Ill Met by Moonlight*, the film Kay had seen with Jack. Bonnie wondered whether he intended inviting her mother to accompany him to the cinema, though merely told him Kay had enjoyed the film.

To her surprise, she noticed her mother enter the

dining room, greet the family who were already halfway through their meal, then head for Charlie's table. None of the couples were down yet.

"Mum, is everything all right?"

Diane nodded. "I thought I'd come and tell you that was the Police on the line. It appears that couple who did the moonlight flit last weekend have been picked up on the South Coast. Obviously, the officer couldn't reveal the details, but the good news is, eventually we should get back at least some of the money they owed."

"Oh, Mum, that's such good news," Bonnie said. "Especially as they'll no longer be able to get up to their nasty tricks."

"Yes, excellent news, Diane. I'm pleased for you," Charlie said. "Um, will the police officer be calling to see you any time soon?"

At once Bonnie took special note of their guest. He'd buttered a piece of toast and held it in his left hand, while the right hand was scrunching his white linen napkin into a ball. What was worrying the man? And did her mother realise his discomfort?

Diane was nodding. "The officer wants to show me a photograph of Mr and Mrs White, but I asked him not to call until after the breakfasts are finished." She glanced at the door. "There's the couple in Room 5 arriving. I'd better get back. Hope your day goes well, Charlie. I'll see you later."

Bonnie went to greet the new arrivals and assure them they could sit at their favourite corner table. But as she went to fetch their coffee, she couldn't help notice Charlie Hamilton wipe his brow with his now extremely crumpled napkin. It was almost as if he was suffering from a guilty conscience.

And as soon as he finished his meal, instead of taking his morning newspaper through to the residents' lounge, he went straight upstairs, only to reappear a few minutes later, carrying his briefcase.

In the hallway, he smiled at Bonnie. "Busy day today, so I'm away a bit earlier than usual. The early bird catches the worm, you know!"

Bonnie saw him out. He walked down the path with his typical jaunty air, but did he think she was a fool? She knew very well he purposely didn't visit his clients too early in the morning. So why suddenly change his tune? Once again, he didn't want to be around when the police officer called. More than ever, Bonnie needed Patrik to reassure her he hadn't got himself mixed up in some crooked racket. Her one o'clock meeting with the young Hungarian couldn't come quickly enough.

"This is one of those days when I miss having a man around the place." Diane was bringing in the empty laundry basket.

"What's up?" Bonnie gave her mother a sympathetic look.

"I've just noticed the downpipe coming away from the wall."

"Can't you ask Sam to send someone round?"

"I don't like asking Sam because he never lets me pay for anything."

Bonnie nodded, well aware her mother liked to retain her independence as much as possible. She thought of Patrik, except she wasn't ready to confess her true feelings to her mother, also he must already have difficulty in juggling two jobs, not to mention the weekly washing of taxis.

As if Diane had opened a window into her daughter's mind, she said, "How about that Hungarian lad you've met? Would he like to earn a bit of cash, I wonder?"

Bonnie willed herself not to blush. "Um, I could ask

him, I suppose. If he's unable to do it, maybe one of his friends could help."

"I'd like to get it looked at while the weather's still so good and I don't think it requires a master craftsman's attention. Shall I leave it with you then, Bonnie?" Her mother gave her a mischievous look. "Only if you're likely to see Patrik soon."

"As it happens, I was planning to see him at lunchtime today."

Diane smiled. "I did wonder, after you told me you were meeting a friend for lunch."

Bonnie raised her eyes to the ceiling. "Mum, don't go getting any ideas, please. Patrik's lovely, but who knows how long he'll be around? It would be awful if we became fond of one another when he'll have to up sticks at the end of the season."

Her mother's smile was gentle. "Sometimes in life we need to enjoy the moment, daughter dear. And I'm sure Patrik must miss his home comforts, so if you ever want to invite him round to tea, he'll be very welcome."

"That's a lovely thought, but Patrik's shifts vary and it's probably best not to complicate things just now."

Diane nodded. "It breaks my heart to think of what he and so many young men like him have had to endure. Does he ever mention his parents?"

Bonnie shook her head, her thoughts whirling like a confetti storm. She'd sensed how painful it was for Patrik to discuss the awfulness of the Hungarian uprising and didn't want to say too much to her mum. Although longing to confide her misgivings over Charlie Hamilton and whether Patrik was at risk, she daren't because she was still uncertain of Diane's feelings about the salesman. Why did life suddenly have to become so complicated?

He arrived at the café on time. Bonnie needed to take a very deep breath indeed as her pulse rate registered Patrik's effect on her emotions. He wore his work clothes of course, but his glossy dark hair and handsome sun-tanned face were what she focused upon as he made his way across the café to spend his afternoon break with her. Straightaway, he took one of her hands in his and kissed the back of it.

"Hello." Bonnie smiled at him. "I hope it's all right with you, but I ordered two cups of coffee and a plate of ham and chips. My treat. I had a very late cooked breakfast so I won't need anything to eat."

He pulled out the chair opposite and sat down. "I don't know what to say, Bonnie, except I don't like to think of you spending your money on me." He gave her a wry smile. "But I am grateful for your kindness. One day I hope the sock may be on the other foot."

She couldn't help chuckling. "I'm sure the boot will be on the other foot one day, Patrik. And quite honestly, if I was the one in your position, I'm sure you'd do the same for me. So there!"

"I think the dungarees would suit you, but not sure about the boots," he said, totally straight-faced.

They laughed together like old friends and Bonnie wished she didn't have to bring up this matter that concerned her so. She sat back as the waitress brought their coffees and put a plate of succulent ham and freshly-fried chips before her. "Do you want another portion now?" the girl asked.

"No, just the one, thanks." She waited until the waitress moved away then pushed the plate towards Patrik. "I'll maybe pinch a chip or two but you start on that while I talk to you about something that affects you. Please believe me when I say I'm only doing this because … well, because I care about you."

He nodded. "I too care about you, Bonnie. Say whatever you want to say to me." He selected a plump golden chip and held it out to her, his fingers brushing hers as she accepted the morsel. "I too have something to discuss."

"Goodness! Well, I hope I can help. Shall I go first?"

"Please."

The words were difficult to find, but she was determined to confess her fears about Mr Hamilton's integrity. Patrik listened carefully while he ate and Bonnie noticed how he concentrated on his plateful of food, stopping to offer her a chip now and then while absorbing every word she said.

"Does that make sense? I tried to find the right words and not beat about the bush."

"That is expression I learnt only recently." He took a sip of coffee. "Thank you for telling me this. I have my own opinion of Mr Hamilton and..." He hesitated. "I am not happy that this other business he manages is, I think you say, above board."

Bonnie cradled her coffee cup in her hands. "You may make the odd mistake, but your English is improving day by day. Well done. Look, Patrik, if we're both right, and I've a horrible feeling we are, that would explain why Mr Hamilton seems so reluctant to be in the house when he finds out someone from the police is due to call. It beats me why he acts like that unless he has something to hide." She bit her lip. "For a while, I even wondered whether he was involved with that couple who did the moonlight flit!"

She saw the expression on Patrik's face. "I mean the couple who left in the night without paying what they owed my mother for a week's accommodation."

"Ah, I see. That was the honeymoon couple." He'd almost cleared his plate. "So that is called a moonlight flit? I shall remember that expression."

"But how can we prove anything? I can't help wondering whether we're worrying about nothing. The man has been staying with us on and off for several years. He's obviously involved in a second business, but why do I feel like I do? Maybe his wanting to avoid the police is due to something entirely different? Perhaps he's been caught speeding recently or was pulled over for some reason and got a severe ticking off by an officer. Often people associate a policeman at the door with being the bearer of bad news."

She knew she was gabbling. Bonnie locked gazes with Patrik and sighed. "No, it doesn't sound convincing, does it? I'm probably on the wrong track. And I'm sure he had nothing to do with that couple the police caught. I was just over-reacting. I'm going to keep quiet and see what you have to say now."

Patrik nodded. "My big concern is that Mr Hamilton warned me not to tell anyone, not even my brother, that I was going to meet him for a talk. This puzzles me, Bonnie. Why would a man say such a thing, if he had nothing to hide?"

CHAPTER 15

Patrik described how he'd been startled to find someone waiting for him after he walked Bonnie home. How, at first, he feared being robbed, even attacked. He spoke quietly, leaning forward and gazing into Bonnie's eyes as he ignored the background sounds of clattering dishes and chattering customers while the urn bubbled and the toaster pinged. He saw Bonnie's eyes widen. She urged him to go on eating while she contemplated what she'd heard.

"Of course," Patrik continued between mouthfuls. "As soon as I realised who it was, I was happy to talk to him, though I was surprised that he was interested in me and what I'd done before I left Hungary. My college training, I think, impressed him and he said he knew I wanted to try and make a better life for myself."

"That's perfectly understandable and it does you credit."

Patrik smiled. "He asked me to meet him the next day so I agreed. He said he would buy me a meal and I thought he did this to make me want to meet him. The breakfast we ate was good but I was more concerned to hear what work he could offer me. And, you know, I was pleased a man like him was taking an interest in me."

Bonnie nodded. "I've always understood he's a sales representative. I've never heard him mention anything else but that."

"He did not wish for me to tell anyone about this. You are the first person I have said anything to and now I am sorry, because I do not mean you to become involved in anything that is ... is ..."

"Dodgy?" She saw his face and tried again. "You mean anything that might be illegal?"

"That is correct. I may be wrong, but I have now been to the airport with him and to the dockyard with another man who works for him."

Bonnie gasped. "How on earth did you get time off?"

"I swapped some hours with young man I share work with."

"Patrik?" Bonnie leaned across the table. "What did you have to do? I really don't like the sound of this."

He offered her another chip. "I too am suspicious. Each evening I have been out, to the airport or to the docks, there were packages to be moved. Goods arriving either by air or by water. All is packed in boxes and my job is to help carry them to the car."

"It sounds fishy to me! Ah, no, Patrik – that's a saying we use when we think something doesn't seem right. I don't think there are flights in or out of Faircliff Airport after about eight o'clock."

"I saw no peoples around except the man who Charlie introduced me to. There were not many lights on either. Not like a big airport."

"I've never flown, but I went there once with Kay's parents when she came back from a visit to her penfriend in Paris. That was a Saturday lunchtime. I can only think there must be a very good reason why you were taken there by night. Same thing with the docks."

Patrik shivered. "Ah, I am not enjoying the docks by night. I'm a good swimmer, but it could be dangerous to wander round with so much water unprotected. Is that the right word?"

"It's a very good word. I've had trips on the paddle steamers and I remember there wasn't any fencing along one side of the quay. You'd need to keep a tight rein on small children if you took them there."

"I don't know what to do now, Bonnie."

"I hope you don't mind my asking, but has Mr Hamilton paid you yet for what you've done?"

"Not yet. He told me he would see me the next time. He'll let me know when that is. I don't want to get into trouble. I can stand up for myself, but I feel very helpless about what I might have got myself into. All the time I keep telling myself, why would such a kind gentleman put me at risk while telling me he wants to help me better myself?"

"I hate to say this, Patrik, but if he really is dealing in contraband goods, it's a very serious matter indeed. You know – handling items that should pass through Customs when they're coming in from a foreign country?"

Patrik felt his stomach churn. "You really do think this is what is going on?"

She nodded. "I'm afraid it sounds highly likely. Everyone likes Charlie Hamilton and I can understand you being keen to earn some extra money, but not this way. We have to get you out of this mess, Patrik. We really do. Before it's too late."

He stared back at her, hating the concern he saw in her lovely blue eyes and knowing he was causing her distress. But as to what he did next, he had absolutely no idea. And a little part of him still wanted to believe in Charlie's honesty.

Bonnie's mother had told her to take as long as she needed. So, after she walked back to the Waltzer with

Patrik, she took the road leading round to the pebbly beach the other side. It was usually quieter than the golden sands which attracted so many families with young children. She climbed the grassy slope up to the cliff top, enjoying the familiar view and looking forward to descending through woodland to reach yet another cove. All the time she walked, she tried to think of some way of helping Patrik stay out of trouble.

The handsome Hungarian, as she'd heard her mother refer to him as, when talking to Kay, was at such a disadvantage, compared to a man like Charlie. From the little he'd said, Bonnie knew Patrik came from a solid family background and his parents had been well-respected members of the community. Now, he held the status of a young foreign man forced to leave behind possessions which would have been so useful to him, had he been able to bring them when fleeing his homeland.

If Charlie was involved in dubious trading and was found out, didn't that mean any employee of his would be incriminated too? Patrik had no means of employing a lawyer to help his plea of ignorance. What if he ended up in prison? Bonnie descended the last few steps, her feet landing on the soft grass above the lip of pebbles flattening out towards the shoreline. She settled herself on a nearby bench and gazed at the gentle waves lapping against the sand, showing where the pebbles ran out, knowing she'd never tire of watching the sea. Patrik was learning to love his new surroundings and she smiled as she pictured them both, walking hand in hand across the sand at low tide, maybe stealing a kiss, laughing when a mischievous breeze whipped Bonnie's curls across her mouth as Patrik lowered his lips towards hers.

Her dream lover pushed her hair away from her face, so tenderly her heart bumped a little faster. Could she hear him murmur those three little words of love? Bonnie closed her eyes then opened them in a flash, wriggling on the wooden bench and scolding herself for avoiding the real reason she'd opted for this solitary thinking time. She jumped as a flock of squawking seagulls flew overhead towards the sea. They were seizing the opportunity to snaffle spoils from a distant paddle steamer heading for the English side of the channel.

At that moment Bonnie decided there could only be one possible solution to Patrik's problem. Even after knowing him for such a short time, she felt sure he wouldn't approve of her suggestion. What's more, he'd probably be cross with her for even thinking about such a thing! But how on earth could she achieve what she wanted without his help?

She rose from the bench and began retracing her footsteps, this time climbing up and away from the restless sea. The wind was strengthening now. Noting the white foam frothing in the distance, Bonnie remembered how she first heard the words 'white horses' used to describe waves breaking. On that occasion, she and her parents were walking on this same pebbly beach. She must have been around seven years of age and she clearly remembered her father stooping down and gently turning her shoulders so she could see what he meant.

She had the strong feeling that her father would have approved of Patrik's courage and determination to do the right thing, despite the dreadful experiences he'd endured. But her dad wasn't here to advise either her or her boyfriend and if he had been, she wouldn't be agonising as to how her mother might suffer when she discovered her friend Charlie was not all he seemed to be.

Whether it was the fresh air or whether her guardian angel was hovering nearby, Bonnie suddenly thought of family friend Sam. He knew so many people in the town, he might be able to provide the information she needed. And even if she angered Patrik by her intervention in his personal life, she would at least have done her best to help him untangle himself from a potentially dangerous situation.

Kay was seated in Diane's rocking chair by the window, mending a torn pillowcase, when Bonnie walked into the kitchen. Golden sunshine bounced light off the copper saucepans and highlighted the auburn tint in her friend's hair. For moments she wished she was artistic, so able to capture the scene in a drawing.

Bonnie looked around her. "Gosh, it's almost three o'clock! I'm so sorry, Kay. I walked further than I meant to and clean forgot Mum was going out to tea this afternoon." She held her wrist to her ear. "And I forgot to wind my watch this morning."

"There's no problem. I'm here until three o'clock anyway so I thought I'd do a bit of mending." She grinned. "Even though I know I'm pinching one of your favourite jobs."

Bonnie groaned. "I'd sooner tackle a mountain of ironing then thread a needle, as you very well know. Anyway, I'm back now if you want to leave a bit early."

"Five more minutes and I'll be through. Did you see Patrik on your travels?"

"Yes, I met him in his break. What about Jack – are you two still keeping your distance?"

Kay pulled a face. "Yes, but to be quite honest, I miss him loads. Yet, I still wonder whether he really wants to go steady, even if he thinks he does. Whereas Patrik seems to be such a faithful, caring kind of person."

"Even after all he's gone through, he always tries to find the best in people."

"There." Kay snipped off a hanging thread and put down the scissors. "I noticed the tear while I was ironing it but this one's for the family linen drawer now."

Bonnie exchanged smiles with her. "I know, Mum has such high standards."

"And look how they've paid off. Ever since I've been helping in the summer holidays, we've seen the bookings increase year by year. She's a good businesswoman is your mum."

Bonnie nodded. "Tell me, Kay. Has she ever said anything to you about Mr Hamilton?"

Kay got up from the rocking chair. "Also known as Lover Boy?"

"What are you saying?"

"Don't tell me you didn't know?"

"Know what? I haven't a clue what you're talking about."

"Mr Hamilton's a regular patron of the Tivoli Tea House. My mum meets her best friend there every Wednesday afternoon and she's seen him turn up with more than one lady over the last weeks. Mind you, he's totally ignored Mum on each occasion. That tells a tale, if you ask me!"

Bonnie's heart was getting a second workout but not for the same reason as the first one. "I didn't know your mum knew him."

"Going back to Easter, he was making a call at Joe's Café while I was working on the Saturday afternoon. Mum came in with my auntie and as he'd recognised me and we were chatting, I thought it'd be rude not to introduce him."

Bonnie knew Kay worked some shifts at the popular promenade café. Charlie Hamilton probably did business with most of the shop and café proprietors along the promenade. And being a good-looking fellow, it was highly likely women would remember meeting him. But this information both concerned and pleased her. If only she knew whether her mum viewed her long-standing guest as a possible marriage partner or as a friend! She'd hate her to get hurt.

"Come on, Bonnie, we both know your mum's not stupid. I think she must be well aware what he's like, even if she hasn't actually seen him in action."

Bonnie thought back to what her mum had said before she went to the dinner dance. No, Diane wouldn't be heartbroken if she learnt about his romantic activities. But she still regarded him as a friend and would be upset if he was found guilty of illegal dealings. She'd heard her mum talk about the black-market goings on during World War II. What Patrik suspected Mr Hamilton might be doing would result in far worse consequences. And, apart from anything else, the guest house benefited from his custom throughout most of the year.

"You're not worried about her, are you?" Kay was on her way to collect her handbag and cardigan from the cupboard under the stairs.

"It's supposed to be the other way around," Bonnie joked. "I just wanted to check, that's all."

"Fair enough." Kay was peering into her hand mirror while applying crimson lipstick. She turned to her friend. "There ... how do I look?"

"Like a J Arthur Rank film starlet!"

Kay collapsed into giggles. "Are you comparing me to Diana Dors?" She stuck her chest out and sashayed across the room, stopping to toss back her hair in a theatrical gesture.

Bonnie applauded. "Now, am I right in thinking you

might be hoping to see whether a certain Mr Jack Williams is working this afternoon?"

"You might be." Kay winked at Bonnie. "I don't want him to think I'm checking up on him but I don't want him to decide I'm losing interest either."

"My goodness." Bonnie sighed. "I wish you luck. This romance business gets complicated sometimes. Making the right decisions, I mean."

Kay was ready to go. "You're not having second thoughts about Patrik, are you?"

"No. No, definitely not. Everything's fine."

CHAPTER 16

Patrik watched Bonnie walk away after they said goodbye to each other and he'd squeezed her hand and whispered "Don't worry about me. I have got myself out of worse situations than this one."

"OK, I'll try not to worry and I'll keep an eye open for anything even vaguely suspicious," Bonnie had replied. "See you on Sunday afternoon, fingers crossed!"

But walking back to work, wishing their Sunday date would come around as quickly as the Waltzer whizzed its riders around the circuit, Patrik felt uneasy about his position. Mr Hamilton was currently snapping his fingers and expecting Patrik to rearrange his working hours to suit. It wouldn't surprise him if the other young man working on the Waltzer kicked up a fuss before long.

Last time Patrik asked him to swap shifts, the other lad told him his girlfriend had moaned at him. And Patrik knew the reaction he could expect from his boss if he suspected his Hungarian employee was working elsewhere. He needed to keep both his original jobs and should never have assumed it would be easy, keeping up with another one as well. He realised now how he'd been carried away by promises given by the smooth-tongued businessman. If he wasn't careful, he could even face being arrested if Bonnie's and his misgivings proved accurate.

Patrik was due to finish his shift at eight o'clock that evening. A few minutes before the hour, he suddenly noticed Charlie Hamilton standing some yards away. He caught Patrik's eye and nodded. Patrik waited until his boss disappeared inside the kiosk and watched for Patrik to give him the thumbs-up to say all riders were safely fastened into the cars. Only then could he slip across the concourse to discover what was going on.

Charlie raised an eyebrow. "You're finishing soon?"

Patrik, wondering how the man could possibly know this, gave him a yes.

"Good. You'll find my car parked near the railway station. Try to get away on time, because this is a last-minute job out at the airport. You'll get the money for the work you've done, including tonight's."

Charlie walked away, leaving Patrik to return to the ride and wait until he received permission to finish. There was no sign of the other worker, but suddenly Patrik was facing the awkward situation he'd been dreading.

"Ah, sir, is it all right for me to go now, please?"

His boss shook his head. "Look, mate, how do you expect me to run this show on my own? It won't hurt you to hang on a few minutes until your opposite number gets here, will it?"

Patrik's hopes descended to somewhere in the direction of his boots. He nodded and turned away to deal with a couple of customers looking to ride. He wondered whether the businessman was watching nearby or whether he was already walking back to his car. Either way, Patrik knew he wouldn't get away from the Waltzer on time and there was nothing he could do about it.

While wondering what might happen if he was

required to stay at work because the other lad had gone sick, his oppo, as the boss described him, appeared from nowhere and Patrik received a nod. He set off, walking as quickly as he could, while dodging clusters of happy holidaymakers having fun on the pleasure park.

"You took your time. What's that all about, then?" Charlie fired the words at him as Patrik slid into the passenger seat.

"I am very sorry. The other worker arrived late so it was impossible for me to leave on time."

Charlie was already driving away. "All right. You know, young Matyaz, I had a very good report from Ken about you. Funnily enough, he's hinting about not enjoying the night work like he used to and his missus is moaning about him going out after dark. These ladies, ay? So, how do you fancy moving up a step or two in my organisation? Young, single bloke like you – you're not afraid of unsocial hours, mate, are you? You'd still have time to spend with that pretty girlfriend of yours. More cash coming in and you wouldn't even need to work on the Waltzer. How does that sound?"

Patrik balled his fists either side of him and kept his gaze fixed on the road as Charlie guided the big car towards the airport. The sky looked sulky and the temperature high enough to make the conditions muggy. Patrik's brow was already damp with perspiration and he couldn't help envying Charlie's open-neck sports shirt worn with well-cut grey slacks. He gave the impression money came his way as smoothly as sweet custard pouring from a jug. What if Patrik and Bonnie were overreacting simply because they didn't know enough about the business the sales rep was running?

But could he trust Charlie enough to throw his lot in with him? Doing so would create another problem for him to deal with. Where would he live? His bunk in the caravan would be given to whoever replaced him for the remainder of the season. And he still wasn't convinced Charlie's promise of better things in view was watertight.

"I'll give you time to think about it." Charlie removed his left hand from the steering wheel and tapped his pocket. "Maybe, when you get the money you're owed, it'll help you make a decision. Remember, I run an operation which doesn't need to end like a funfair ride grinding to a halt once the traders shut up shop for the winter."

They drove on in silence, Patrik's thoughts in turmoil. What if Bonnie's and his suspicions were totally unfounded? By turning Charlie down, he might be throwing away the perfect opportunity to boost his savings and improve his chances of applying for the college course he wanted. The weeks were counting down towards the end of the holiday season and Patrik feared being left jobless, while Bonnie, he felt sure, would find a good position in an office either in the town or in nearby Cardiff. He didn't want her to feel sorry for him, but could he totally trust Charlie Hamilton? Nor did he believe the businessman would remain in the town once the holiday season ended.

"You don't have to make your decision tonight." Charlie was slowing the car, ready to drive on to the airport concourse. "Excuse me if I'm speaking out of turn, but I'd have thought our Miss Bonnie Morgan would approve of you trying to better yourself." He directed a sly sideways glance at his passenger.

Patrik frowned. If Charlie knew what Bonnie thought, he wouldn't be quite so confident regarding her feelings. But he had the luxury of more time before he committed himself. "Thank you. Yes. I need to make up my mind and let you know soon, Charlie."

"Good man. I like the cut of your jib, Patrik."

"Um ..." Patrik was at a loss to understand. Some English expressions were still far beyond even his still-improving language skills.

"That means I have confidence in you, mate. I think you need more to keep you occupied than selling tickets to teenagers and making sure they're all strapped in. Not that you don't do a good job on the Waltzer, of course."

He'd negotiated the slip road and parked in his usual spot beside the big hangar. "I have to go across to the Control Tower so you'd better accompany me in case you ever need to come on your own. I need to pick up a document from someone who can't leave his post as the charter flight I'm looking for is due in soon. Better make it snappy!"

Patrik leapt from the car and followed Charlie, who'd begun jogging across the tarmac towards the Control Tower overlooking the runway and surrounding area. He had no idea what was going on and what made this evening different from the other occasions he'd visited. As they hurried across the runway towards the main building, Patrik glanced up at the windows of the tower and saw a man wearing headphones and looking fully-absorbed in whatever he was doing. He felt a surge of excitement as he wondered whether he'd be able to take a look at the operational centre of the airport.

But Charlie opened the nearest door and beckoned to Patrik to follow him inside. Patrik pulled the door closed and followed him down a dingy corridor towards a door at its end. The rattle and tap of some kind of machinery became louder as Charlie knocked then opened the door straightaway. Patrik slipped through and shut the door behind him. A bank of machines faced him and a balding, bespectacled man wearing sports jacket and trousers was peering intently at whatever was being printed on the paper emerging from a big contraption, the likes of which Patrik had never seen before.

Charlie nudged Patrik's elbow as the employee crossed the room and unlocked a filing cabinet. "These things are teleprinters. There's an operator at the other end, probably Bristol Airport in this case, communicating details so the staff here know how many people are on board the flight and what time it took off – stuff like that."

Patrik nodded, interested to learn although deciding it was best not to enquire why the pair of them were standing where they were. But the telex operator was back and with a quick nod to Charlie, handed him a brown envelope which was pocketed at once.

"Thanks, mate. Much obliged." Charlie took a step towards the door then hesitated, turning to face the bespectacled man again. "By the way, this is my colleague, John Davis."

Patrik was much too surprised to protest. What was the businessman up to now and why this false name?

The other man nodded, looked at the big clock on the wall and muttered something to Charlie who thanked him and turned at once to Patrik. "We need to beat it. Now!"

Yet again, Patrik did as he was told. Outside, he realised the wind was getting up and he fell into step with Charlie, only to see his employer set off across the runway as if the hounds of hell were pursuing him. He heard him yell 'Come on!' and suddenly realised he could hear the heavy drone of engines. Engines that meant business. To his horror, a swift glance to his left showed an aeroplane swooping from the sky, its wheels down ready to land. He hadn't felt as though his heart was in his mouth since, escaping Hungary, he was forced to plunge into the murky depths of a river and swim to the other side. At that point he knew his life depended upon getting across the water. Now, again with self-preservation in mind and his legs moving like well-oiled pistons, he caught Charlie up just as the older man stumbled. Luckily Patrik managed to grab his employer's arm and pull him out of the aeroplane's path. Both men stood back and Patrik knew his companion was finding it harder to get his breath back than he was.

He and Charlie had crossed the runway with what felt like moments to spare. Patrik's pulse rate still provided a reminder of how terrified he'd been. His employer's chalk-white face showed his state of mind was none too good either. Patrik stood, watching the sturdy aircraft slowing and eventually stopping not far from the terminal building. The pilot cut the engines and the propellers slowed and stilled while two ground staff pushed a set of steps on wheels towards the rear of the aircraft. Patrik remembered learning what war horses these Dakota had been throughout and since the Second World War.

"Sorry about that, old son." Charlie, sounding his usual jaunty self, took out a comb and smoothed back his hair. "I didn't mean to cut it so fine, but it was important to get my hands upon a certain piece of paperwork before they lock up the Control Tower building. Get it?"

Patrik got it. Or, at least he thought he did. But he still had a big question to ask. "What now. sir? I mean Charlie – and why, please, did you give me another name when you introduced me to that man?"

Charlie chuckled and tapped the side of his nose. "Best leave me to decide these things. John Davis is a common name in Wales while, with respect, your name is so unusual round these parts, it's best not to broadcast it to any Tom, Dick or Harry you meet in the course of your duties.

Patrik nodded, deciding it was pointless making a fuss about something Charlie had obviously thought was the best action to take.

"As for your first question, now we wait for the passengers to disembark. One of the ground staff will taxi the 'plane back to the hangar and we can pick up our consignment then. I need to show the paperwork to the Customs officer dealing with freight inwards then we'll get ourselves a trolley and take the goods to my car and Bob's your uncle."

"You are saying all is well?" Patrik ran one hand through his tousled mop of hair.

"Oh, worry not, old son! All is very well indeed."

CHAPTER 17

Bonnie gazed out of the window and pulled a face. "Was rain forecast, Mum? It's teeming down at the moment."

Diane groaned. "I don't know if it was forecast, but it's such a shame for the holidaymakers, when so many of them save all year round for their summer break."

"At least our guests won't get pushed out of their accommodation like some landladies insist on doing."

"I've always thought that was a horrid thing to do. This week's guests don't seem as sociable as last week's lot but we'll make sure the board games and playing cards are on the table. You never know, it might be a case of rain before seven – fine before eleven." Diane adjusted the gas flame and pushed the grill pan underneath. "I'm just starting the sausages."

Bonnie headed for the door. "I'll pour the orange juice and put my cheerful face on for the guests."

"You're always cheerful, love! No sign of Kay is there? Did she say she'd be in late?"

"Not to me." Straightaway Bonnie remembered how her friend had planned to go to the pleasure park the previous afternoon. But she said nothing to her mother and mentally crossed her fingers that Kay hadn't arrived at The Wall of Death, only to find Jack flirting with a girl, or, worse still, being told he wanted to finish things between them.

"Well, she's such a good worker, I'll give her the benefit of the doubt, but it makes things harder for you if you're waitressing on your own and everyone comes down at the same time. I'll do my best to back you up."

Bonnie set off for the dining room. No one was seated yet, unsurprising on a wet morning, though sometimes guests had already booked for a coach trip and didn't want to miss their excursion. Today nobody appeared to be in a hurry. She poured glasses of juice, taking care not to spill any on the pristine white table linen her mother prided herself on using. She was walking back to the kitchen when she realised Kay had arrived via the back door as usual. Her friend was kitted out for wet weather and stood on the doormat, gingerly removing her raincoat. Her umbrella was already making a small puddle in a corner.

"Poor you." Bonnie went to the cupboard to fetch a towel. "Will this help?"

"Ooh, lovely, thanks. It's horrible out there so I waited for the bus and ended up taking longer than if I'd walked. Sorry I'm late."

Bonnie looked carefully at her. Something was up but Kay seemed calm enough so Bonnie decided not to ask questions in case she placed her friend in an awkward position. After all, not everything could be said in front of a mother.

Kay read Bonnie's expression and did some extreme eye-rolling. Bonnie hastily looked elsewhere before she burst out laughing. The pair of them had kept secrets and shared secrets since they were small girls, best friends and never far from each other's side at primary school then afterwards at grammar school. Whatever Kay had to say could wait. But she definitely didn't seem downcast, even though the rain had turned her auburn fringe a mahogany colour and she was bemoaning the fact that her hair would probably stay frizzy all day now. This was deemed to be a catastrophe. But nor was it unusual and was in fact rather comforting, Bonnie decided.

Charlie Hamilton put his head round the door. "Good morning, ladies. How are you doing?" He didn't wait for an answer. "Looks like I'm the first one down. I have an appointment in the big city today so if one of your couples fancies a ride to the big city, I plan to leave here at nine thirty." He beamed at them. "Now, where's my morning paper?"

"The boy's late this morning, Mr Hamilton. I'll keep an ear open for him and bring it in to you."

"He's probably waterlogged. Thanks, Bonnie."

"We'll make sure to mention your kind offer of transport," Diane said, smiling at their guest.

"It might be just the day to visit a museum or Cardiff Castle. They'll need to find their own way back, but that's not a problem."

Bonnie noticed the dazzling smile he gave her mother while she herself didn't appear to be quite so popular with Mr Hamilton. Could it be he suspected Patrik had told her all about his new job and worried that too many people might find out and possibly put two and two together to make five? If so, she could do nothing about it.

The morning after the airport job took place, on opening his pay packet from the night before, Patrik received a surprise. He hadn't wanted any of his caravan mates to know what was going on so let them assume his absences were due to his new love life. He'd checked his earnings in a rare period when he was on his own because the other three young men were starting work earlier than he was. There was far more cash in the small brown envelope than he'd imagined finding, but he was trying not to let that influence his decision. Possibly the rate varied depended upon how much hanging about and lifting and shifting was involved. And if a job meant working on past midnight, surely that must have a bearing on the payment?

He knew he must open a Post Office savings account. He had no idea when he'd be able to do that but probably first thing in the morning would be best. His brother would tell him how to go about it, so that would mean going to see Istvan or, failing finding him in, asking one of his friends who also lived in the same boarding house. He knew they'd help if Istvan wasn't around to advise him.

Meanwhile Patrik needed to put the money in a safe place. He contemplated walking to *Sea Breezes* and asking Bonnie to keep it for him until their meeting on Sunday. Then he'd just have to put it beneath his pillow that night and take it to the Post Office on Monday morning. It occurred to him Bonnie would probably know what he needed in order to open a savings account so he mightn't even need to bother Istvan who, Patrik knew, was currently working on a very important plumbing job.

His brother was also courting. Istvan had fallen in love with a girl he'd met at a Saturday night dance and hoped to settle down with her and start a family one day. Patrik envied Istvan's determination, even if he thought he was possibly rushing too quickly into an engagement. But he was in a far more secure position than Patrik and was an example of how well you could get on if you had a particular skill.

That was the deciding factor for Patrik. He needed more money so he could buy himself a decent outfit and stop looking as though he'd been rendered homeless, even if that actually was the case. If he crossed his fingers and took up this offer of further employment, he should be able to save hard and once he had enough, could quit working for Charlie and move on. He mustn't think the worst of the businessman, despite Bonnie's concerns. Surely Charlie wouldn't threaten him in some way?

But to his dismay, he'd failed to realise that in order to replace Ken, he'd need a British driving licence. He used to drive his father's car while living at home, but he was unable to drive a car in his new country. This made him feel very disappointed, also curious as to why this matter wasn't mentioned when he'd been offered more work. It didn't make sense. Unless Charlie Hamilton really was a man completely without scruples. A man who would ignore laws and regulations in order to achieve what he wanted. Patrik hoped he'd been mistaken when assuming this might involve being given a forged driving permit.

Mr Hamilton set off with an elderly couple who'd jumped at the chance of a lift to the city. Diane was obviously pleased by his generosity and alarmed Bonnie by saying more than once how thoughtful he was to make such a kind gesture, and what a pleasure it was to have him stay in the guesthouse. Bonnie, fearful of what she might find out about their model guest's business methods, wondered how her mother would react if forced to realise Charlie wasn't the man whose polite, charming façade apparently fooled so many people.

For the other guests' sakes, Bonnie was relieved when the rain stopped mid-morning as her mother had hoped. The tea towels which had been boiling in an old pan on the gas stove could be rinsed and hung outside to dry. If she took on this task, she felt certain Kay would slip out for a quick chat.

Bonnie finished putting the towels through the mangle and carried them outside to the line. Her mother was on the phone in the hallway and Kay wasted no time in popping outside.

"I've finished washing up, but I'm not sure what your mum wants me to do next." Kay said. "So, I thought I'd come and talk to you."

"Thank goodness! Are you going to tell me how you got on with Jack, before I expire from curiosity?"

Kay handed her a couple of clothes pegs. "He looked delighted to see me and told me he'd have called round this evening if I hadn't come to the ride. Mum and Dad have been invited to play cards with my auntie and uncle so they'll be out for the evening. I've asked Jack to come to my house."

"Goodness! Are you sure your parents won't mind?"

Kay shrugged. "Dunno. I mightn't tell them. It'll be lovely to have some time on our own. I'll take him into the front room so we can listen to my Pat Boone records."

"Kay…. you will be careful, won't you?"

Her friend watched her peg the last tea towel on the line and faced her, arms folded. "What do you take me for, Bonnie? I thought you'd be pleased for me, but maybe you're jealous because you can't invite Patrik round here without falling over the guests? And who could blame them for thinking he was an odd job man come to do some work?"

Bonnie stared at her, dismayed. Horrified even. "Look, I'm pleased for you, of course I am, but isn't it a bit soon for you to – you know, be totally alone with him. You and Jack haven't spent all that much time together since he asked you out."

"Precisely. It's time we did, so please don't feel you

have to call round and chaperone us. I'm not sixteen years old, you know. I have a horrible feeling you've been listening to gossip. So, Jack's had several girlfriends since we used to go out together? That doesn't mean he treated any of them badly. We drifted apart and now we're together again."

With that, she picked up the laundry basket and stalked back to the kitchen. Bonnie stood, wondering why she was so touchy. How far would she go to please Jack and keep him interested in her? But Kay had touched a raw nerve all right. Bonnie and Patrik were unable to spend much time together because he was juggling two jobs and the only place she could entertain him was the kitchen.

Bonnie tried her best to keep out of the way for the rest of the morning. She and her mother and Kay always shared a pot of tea and a plate of sandwiches around two o'clock, after which Kay left to put in her hours at the promenade café. Today, as she had an errand to see to, Bonnie wanted to ask her mother if she'd be at home. Kay was still very quiet and if Diane noticed an atmosphere between the two girls, she didn't mention it.

Kay and Bonnie left the guest-house at the same time.

"I suppose you're off to see Patrik?" Kay said once they were walking down the hill.

"No, as it happens, I'm after some advice and I'm hoping Mum's friend, Sam, can help me."

"OK. You don't want to talk to me about anything?"

"Um, it's a bit ticklish. Sorry, but it's probably best not to say anything at the moment."

"Fine. You expect me to tell you everything that's going on in my life, but when it comes to yours, I obviously can't be trusted!"

Bonnie tried to take Kay's arm but her friend kept on walking. "Kay, please don't get in a huff."

That stopped Kay in her tracks. "This is all to do with our Hungarian friend, isn't it? You've gone all starry-eyed over Patrik but he's not ideal boyfriend material, is he? His hours seem to be worse than Jack's and he stays in a scruffy caravan."

Bonnie was about to protest but Kay wouldn't be stopped. "Of course, it's sad how he had to leave his country and lost so much, but why don't you admit you're pining over him? Face it, Bonnie! He's in a shaky position and I think you ought to know your mum told me she was worried about you becoming too involved."

"You've been discussing Patrik with Mum?" Bonnie felt a wave of frustration. "If you really must know, he has a problem at the moment and I'm trying to help him solve it. And, madam, if he'd only been able to stay in his own country, he'd still be on the way to qualifying as an opthalmo...op...oh heck, whatever it is he was training to be. And he might be stuck in a scruffy caravan, but I bet he has a better brain that Jack has. So there!"

Bonnie held her breath. Back to the playground. Back to one breaktime when she'd been jealous because her best friend had gone off to play a skipping game, hand in hand with another little girl, totally ignoring Bonnie. But this time the cause of the row was a tall, handsome young man, not a little girl in pigtails.

"Perhaps," Kay said in a tone that would freeze a sand castle, "it'll be a good thing when the season ends. You and I won't have to see each other then. In fact, we won't have to see each other ever again!"

With that, she marched off down the hill. Bonnie stood watching until her friend disappeared from view and she felt calm enough to go on walking. But she felt a huge wave of sadness. They'd had minor spats before, mostly on the same level as their daft little playground tiff, but this time feelings cut deeper. They were young women with grown-up emotions and values and Bonnie knew she must have things out with her mum. If Charlie Hamilton proved to be a villain in a smart three-piece suit, then she was sorry, but Diane must be made aware of his true nature.

CHAPTER 18

Mr Booker's builder's yard was a half hour walk. Bonnie almost caught a bus but decided to calm herself before confiding her concerns to Sam. He'd been Uncle Sam to her throughout her childhood and he and his late wife were a great help and comfort to the little family when Bonnie's father was pronounced lost at sea.

As she grew older and with both Sam and her mother widowed, Bonnie used to hope the two would marry so she'd have a daddy again. But she thought Sam lacked the confidence to court Diane Morgan and once Charlie Hamilton appeared on the scene, Bonnie realised her mum was bowled over by him although it took a long while before he got around to asking her out.

But that afternoon, all Bonnie wanted was to ask Sam to help her find answers to issues which puzzled her. He'd always lived in the town, knew all the local traders and had worked for, also employed, many local people. His successful business resulted from hours and hours of hard work, helped by the opportunity to construct a much-needed post-war estate of pre-fab houses at the opposite end of the town from the beach.

She arrived at the yard and tapped on the office building's door with no response. She waited a while before knocking again. If Sam wasn't there, surely his secretary would surface? Moments later the boss himself opened the door, trailing flex and balancing the phone in one hand while he held the receiver clamped to one ear. His thick mop of black curls was threaded with silver these days and his tanned skin showed how much time he spent outdoors.

He beamed at her as though she'd made his day, then mouthed 'take a seat,' as he moved back to his desk. Bonnie closed the door and sat down in the chair facing him, keeping her gaze fixed on her hands clasped in her lap.

Sam finished his call. He looked at her, his eyes narrowed, and she knew he was well aware this wasn't a social call. "Well, this is a pleasant surprise, Miss Morgan. I imagine you're here because of some problem?"

She nodded. "Hello, Mr Booker. Yes, I could do with some advice if you can spare the time."

"I always have time for you, Bonnie. Even if my secretary's left, leaving me high and dry."

Bonnie gasped. "Oh, no. When did she leave, Sam?"

"About two hours ago! Anyway, go on my dear. You don't need my problems. And how's your mum? It's not the guttering again, is it?"

"No, the guttering's fine and so is Mum, thanks. Well, she mentioned something about the down pipe, but that's not why I need your advice."

Sam was looking at her enquiringly, leaning back in his chair. She had to bite the bullet.

"The thing is, I've become friendly with one of the Hungarian refugees. His name is Patrik Matyaz and he works on the funfair – on the Waltzer."

Sam's eyes twinkled. "Is this young man a friend or are you telling me he's your boyfriend?"

"Since you ask, he's very special to me. But you'll understand, after what Patrik's gone through, he's in very much reduced circumstances. From the little he's said, I know he comes from a good family, but his parents are both dead and the family home burned down. He and his elder brother and some friends had to leave in a hurry. Patrik and Istvan made it to South Wales."

Sam nodded. "I'm sorry. I've had dealings with Istvan Matyaz. He's an excellent plumber. So, Patrik's his brother?"

"Yes." Bonnie leaned forward just as Sam's phone rang.

"Typical! Be an angel and make us both a cuppa, would you? While I take this call."

In the secretary's office Bonnie took the kettle through to the little washroom and filled it. Back in the office, she checked the fridge and to her surprise, found a bottle of still fresh milk plus a packet of chocolate digestive biscuits. While waiting for the kettle to boil, she wondered how Sam would manage without anyone manning the office.

He was writing in his work book as she appeared beside him with a cup of tea and a biscuit on a small, very battered tin tray.

"Two sugars still, I hope?"

"You bet." He grinned at her. "That call was someone asking me to give an estimate to build a house on a prime plot of land up at the top end of town. Could be a lucrative job. How much would it take to tempt you away from working for your mum?" He burst out laughing. "Only joking! You should see your face, young Bonnie."

"Actually, Sam, you might be joking, but the way things are going, I could well consider accepting your offer." To her horror, the tears she'd been dreading suddenly had their wicked way with her and Bonnie's sobs wracked her slender frame while Sam got to his feet, having produced a large, clean white handkerchief which he handed to her before going into the other office and returning with another mug of tea.

"No sugar, if I remember rightly." He put his hand on her shoulder. "Let it all out, lovey. I'm here when you're ready to talk. And don't you worry about anything getting back to Diane. Nor do I shock easily."

After several sobs followed by mopping of eyes and nose blowing, Bonnie heaved a big sigh and picked up her cup of tea. "Thanks, Uncle Sam. I'll launder your hanky and return it to you." She managed a tremulous smile.

"Uncle Sam? Blimey, that takes me back a year or four. It's good to see a smile on your face again, young lady." He looked at the clock on the wall. "I'm all yours for the next twenty minutes, then I have someone coming for a job interview."

"For the secretary's job? Already?"

"No, I'll need to advertise that one in the local paper. I need more site workers."

Bonnie's brain moved into gear and she wondered whether Patrik might be suitable. If only he didn't have this worrying obligation …

"I'm not sure where to start with all this," she said.

"At the beginning would be good." Sam sat back in his chair, gave her a mischievous look and dunked his biscuit in his tea.

"A while back, I literally bumped into Patrik at the fun fair. We got chatting." She explained how the evening progressed and how Patrik walked her home and her mother's favourite guest met them, having offered to go and look for her after hearing about the fire at the Wall of Death.

Bonnie tried to be concise so Sam got the full picture

but she was unable to explain why she didn't trust Charlie Hamilton. "He's been staying with us for years on and off, but this summer he's turned into a permanent resident," she said. "When he offered Patrik some work, I was surprised, but when I found out a bit more about it, I began to worry."

Sam listened while Bonnie described Patrik's outings with Charlie, also with a man called Ken.

Here, Sam sat up straight and frowned at her. "Do you know Ken's other name?"

"Sorry, Patrik didn't say. He probably wasn't told it. But now Ken's wanting to give up night time work, Mr Hamilton's offered more hours to Patrik. Obviously, he can do with the money but he's worried something illegal might be going on and these goods are being imported without the proper procedures being followed."

"And if our friend Hamilton's caught, you're afraid he'll take Patrik down with him?"

She nodded. "It sounds as though he doesn't want to let Patrik go. I wouldn't put it past him to stir things up and make trouble if Patrik refuses to play ball. Then he'd lose his job on the Waltzer also his accommodation, even if it's only a caravan bunk." She sighed. "There's something else, too."

"I think I can guess. Diane's sweet on Hamilton, isn't she?" Sam picked up a pencil and jabbed it into his work book. "I suspected as much when I called once and he turned up with his suitcase and presented your mum with a bunch of flowers. Made me feel a chump for not thinking of doing that myself. He's a smooth devil, if you don't mind my saying so. I'd hate to see your mum hurt, but I can understand why she's taken to him."

"Kay and I both know Mun's not daft enough to believe she's the only one he pays attention to. Kay's mum's seen him out with more than one glamorous lady, apparently."

Bonnie watched Sam's face and suddenly realised Sam's true feelings about her mother. How long had he felt like this? Everyone knew he'd taken a long while to recover from the loss of his wife. This summer, Sam's son was away fruit picking with chums, somewhere in France, while his father was on his own and now lacking a secretary too. Bonnie knew what she must do.

"If you'll have me, I'd love to help you out for the rest of the summer, at least. My secretarial skills could do with brushing up and come September I'll start applying for a full-time position with prospects. You could advertise your job vacancy and include a starting date if you like."

Sam was staring at her, open-mouthed. "But what about *Sea Breezes*? Your mum'll never speak to me again if I poach you, especially halfway through the season. Is that friend of yours still working with you?"

"Kay's still with us, and you wouldn't be being disloyal to Mum. She has several people who've come in to help her before and who'd still be willing to work a few hours a day. Mum knows I need to find the right job before the winter sets in." She shook her head. "To be honest, Kay and I have had a massive falling out, but I'm hoping we can put it behind us." She twisted a stray tendril of hair around one finger. "Now, how can I best explain why we argued, I wonder?"

"Boyfriend trouble?"

"Kind of. I worry about Kay and Jack. She worries about me and Patrik, but it's a different kind of worry." Bonnie knew she was blushing, but she wasn't about to confide her fear about Jack having only one thing on his mind when he arrived to spend the evening alone with Kay. And it had nothing to do with her beloved collection of Pat Boone records.

"Would I know this young man?"

"Jack Williams. His parents run the corner shop on Queen's Road?"

"Of course. He's a mechanic, isn't he? I called in the shop last week and Jack's dad was moaning about his son working at the Wall of Death when he should be looking for a respectable position in a garage."

Bonnie was aware Sam knew loads of people in the town, but she wanted to return to the subject of the man called Ken. "If Patrik can find out what Ken's surname is, may I give you a ring to see if you know him?"

"Not so fast, Bonnie. I have a feeling I know what his name is already." He leaned forward again. "Does he drive a black Morris Minor?"

Bonnie thought for a moment. "Yes, I'm sure Patrik mentioned that make of car. He said both Mr Hamilton and this chap Ken have collected him in a Morris Minor. I think the car Charlie uses for his normal day visits is a Jaguar. It's certainly a big, flashy red motor car so he must keep the little black one for these jobs on the side."

"A nice, commonplace motor that isn't eye-catching, whereas Lover Boy drives a Jaguar, ay?" He caught Bonnie's eye.

"Kay used the same expression," she said wistfully. "Lover Boy, I mean. She does make me laugh."

"Hey, don't be so glum. The pair of you will make it up. You've fallen out because you're both having man trouble. It makes a change from squabbling over who's been given the best part in the school play or has the most signatures in their autograph book."

"You're right of course, but I'd hate to think Kay would go along with what Jack wanted, just to please him." She hesitated. "Going back to what you asked me, do you actually know someone called Ken who drives a

Morris car?"

Sam nodded, face solemn. "If it's the same Ken I suspect it is, I know his wife's fidgeting about him doing odd jobs at night. She's a thoroughly nice woman and she used to sing in the same church choir as my late wife. We use the same greengrocer and her husband's erratic hours were very much on her mind last time I saw her. But I never dreamt he might be earning spare cash by dishonest means. That really is sailing close to the wind and from what you tell me about Patrik's experiences, the sooner he gets out of Hamilton's clutches, the better it'll be for him."

Bonnie was trying to gather courage to ask Sam if he'd consider giving Patrik a job interview when he stood up and pulled his jacket from the back of his chair. "Sorry, Bonnie, but I have to be ready for my two candidates."

Her hopes fizzled out. She was too late. Sam was a kind man but she couldn't expect preferential treatment, especially now he'd shortlisted two young men as possible workers.

"I'm delighted you called, Bonnie. If you like, I can pop round to see your mum once you've explained everything to her – make sure she's happy with your idea, because I certainly am."

"That'll be great. I'll explain it to her and reassure her we'll give her time to take on someone she trusts. What if I put in a couple of hours here tomorrow afternoon as soon as I'm free? I can learn my way round your filing system and take phone calls if you have to go out."

He beamed. "Perfect. And I hope things improve for your Patrik. I'll let you know if I hear of any jobs going in the town that might suit him."

"Thanks, Sam."

As he opened the outer door for her, Bonnie could have sworn she heard him start to hum *Love Letters in the Sand*. There was sadness in those lyrics, though. Had Sam once written love letters to Diane in the sand? Been pipped at the post by Bonnie's handsome seafaring father? She would love to know the truth about his feelings. Especially now each of them had been widowed some years. But could nice, sensible Sam compete with the man her mother seemed to find so interesting?

CHAPTER 19

Patrik knew he was pushing his luck by not jumping at Charlie's offer of more work. Despite promising him he needn't make up his mind at once, Patrik returned to the caravan to find a note for him, pushed under the caravan door.

He was so looking forward to spending a rare free evening with Bonnie, Patrik deliberately tore up the note and put the pieces in the rubbish bin, burying them beneath tea leaves and orange peel. He pushed away forebodings about the consequences of this action, determined to stick to his arrangements. Patrik was going to Istvan's place for a shower and his brother was lending him a set of clothes. It was fortunate the two were about the same size and Patrik was quite prepared to tell Bonnie he was wearing a borrowed outfit, knowing she was a kind girl who understood his position. He also knew Istvan, who'd been urging him to find himself a job while he was still in one, would ask what progress his younger brother was making.

Sure enough, Istvan sat on the end of his bed while Patrik put on the clean clothing, scolding him in their own language. "Your English is much improving, you know. It is probably better than mine. You need to go to visit the Employment Exchange. Ask your girlfriend to go with you in case you need help. She sounds a good girl. I am pleased for you but you mustn't hang about. Take any job you think you can handle and worry about the next step after that. I know you want to be back at college, but you need to be patient."

Patrik had pretended not to notice tears glistening in his brother's eyes as he gave his pep talk. They both knew the advice was exactly what their father would have given, had he still been around. Patrik promised to speak to Bonnie, also to ask her about opening a post office account.

"That is good," Istvan agreed. "Take your identity card with you and explain all your other documents were lost in a fire. Now get out of here and take your young lady somewhere you can have fun. We all need fun in our lives, little brother. I'm taking my fiancée to the cinema and I need to leave here very soon. You better keep that outfit I lent you, in case you get asked to attend interview."

Patrik gave Istvan a hug, feeling guilty at still not finding the courage to confide his fears. He was still trying to forget that torn up note back in the caravan and wouldn't put it past Charlie to turn up just as he was collecting Bonnie. In his suddenly carefree mood at the thought of a night off with his beautiful girlfriend, Patrik had forgotten Charlie might well be at the guesthouse when Patrik arrived. So, it was not without foreboding that he rang the *Sea Breezes* doorbell at exactly seven o'clock.

Bonnie answered his knock almost immediately. She stood, taking in Patrik's smart, casual clothing then looked more closely at his hair. "You look different."

He chuckled. "In a good way, I hope. I visited a barber. And you look beautiful, Bonnie. Shall we promenade?" He held out his hand to her and she closed the door and placed her hand in his.

"I can't believe we haven't had to postpone our date," Bonnie said, leaning her head towards him.

Patrik breathed in her scent. "That is a beautiful perfume. It smells of flowers but I don't know their name."

"The scent is Freesia. I'm glad you like it." She squeezed his hand. "I have lots to tell you. Where did you plan on going this evening?"

"Well, what do you know!"

An unwelcome intruder. Both Bonnie and Patrik stopped walking and turned to face the speaker.

Charlie Hamilton made a mock bow. "Well, well. Having a night out, are you? But did you not receive my note, Patrik?"

Patrik steeled himself to face up to the older man. Bonnie grabbed his hand as if to reassure him she was on his side.

"What note?" Patrik frowned slightly.

"The note I slid beneath the door of your caravan. Don't tell me you haven't been back there?"

Patrik seized the chance to avoid an actual lie. "I showered and changed at my brother's place and came straight from there to collect Bonnie."

"My, my ... and don't you both look a picture. I hate to spoil the party, but the fact is, Patrik, I need your help tonight." He turned to Bonnie. "You'll understand, won't you, sweetheart? Your boyfriend can earn good money, working with me."

"To be honest, his company's more important to me than his money, Mr Hamilton." Bonnie's tone was frosty. This man might be a favourite of her mother's but she wasn't about to go home again, nor did she expect Patrik to jump through hoops. But her tummy lurched as she wondered just how low Charlie would stoop to get his own way.

"Sir, I have an arrangement to take Bonnie out this evening and it is not possible to let her down. I am sorry I cannot help you." Patrik spread his hands in a gesture of regret.

"You place me in a very awkward position." Charlie looked at Bonnie. "I'd like a word in private with Patrik, if you'll forgive me."

Bonnie looked at Patrik who gave her a brief nod of agreement. She bit her lip but walked a few paces down the slope.

Patrik didn't flinch as Charlie turned to him and gripped his arm. "It wouldn't be very pleasant if you suddenly found you'd lost your fairground job, now would it my friend? I have plenty of useful contacts, old son. Do you get my drift?"

Patrik drew himself up to his full height. "Are you threatening me?"

Charlie grinned. "I find you far too useful to let you slip out of my hands. And how do I know you'll hold your tongue, given some of my dealings are, shall we say, sometimes not quite within the required regulations."

Patrik gasped. He'd suspected as much and now he knew it was true. But would anybody believe him?

"Ken's not the man he used to be. I haven't time to recruit someone else. Will you come with me, or do I have to go on my own?"

Patrik knew his future hung in the balance.

Bonnie was fuming. She felt sure Patrik was under pressure and could well decide it best not to annoy the businessman by refusing to do what he wanted. If she didn't act now, her boyfriend could become more and more immersed in a dark world where he'd be at the mercy of someone else's greed. She turned and ran back up the slope.

Charlie Hamilton glared at her. "Push off! Do you

want your mother to lose the business I give her, as well as lose your darling boyfriend? Because that's what'll happen, when he's jobless and homeless!"

Bonnie didn't move an inch, even though she itched to tell Charlie how interested her mum would be to hear of his behaviour.

For moments, Patrik seemed frozen to the pavement. Then, holding his head high, he addressed the angry businessman. "I have said my piece. I am not happy with the kind of work you offer and I no longer wish to be involved. Thank you for thinking of me, but now, I need to take my girlfriend out to supper."

He reached for Bonnie's hand and without a backward glance, the couple set off down the hill.

"I'm still shaking," Bonnie whispered as they walked. "But you were brilliant. You really stood up to him. You even thanked him!"

"It had to be said. I made a mistake in the beginning when I accepted his offer, but now I can be free of him. Even if he gets me dismissed from the Waltzer, I shall sleep on my brother's floor if necessary – take any job I can find, like Istvan advised me."

"Your brother sounds great. Maybe I can meet him some time."

Patrik longed to look round and see whether Charlie had moved on though resisted the temptation. "I'm wearing his clothes this evening, but before too long, I hope to be making an honest living and boarding somewhere comfortable. Life in the caravan is not ideal."

"Patrik, you don't need to buy a meal. But I want to talk something through with you. Shall we find a quiet café?"

"But I wish to buy you a cocktail or whatever drink you like?"

"That's sweet of you, but I need to keep a clear head. If we go to Joe's café it shouldn't be too busy at this time. And afterwards, I'd like to have some fun. Ride the scenic railway – jump on the ghost train. Act like a couple of kids!"

"You would certainly get on well with my brother. OK. You win. And you can begin talking to me as we walk." He put his arm around her waist.

Bonnie began by explaining who Sam was. She described how she'd offered to help him out with the office work and Patrik nodded his head.

"That sounds sensible. But what about your work at your mother's guest house?"

"We'll easily find someone else. But there are a few maintenance problems and she could do with a handyman." Bonnie hoped he wouldn't feel as though she regarded him as a charity case.

"Mum told me she can't ask Sam for help because he'll insist on carrying out the repairs for nothing. I wonder, now you've turned down Charlie Hamilton's work, if you might be interested in a few hours here and there? Mum's happy for me to ask you."

Patrik took so long to reply, she was afraid he'd taken offence.

"I would be honoured to help. But I am not trained as a carpenter, or a plumber like my brother."

"It's minor repairs and you could come and take a look before you say yes."

She'd made him smile. And drop a kiss on the top of her head, sending warm tingles down her backbone.

"I shall be honoured to. Please thank your mother for me."

"I will. Now, how about we forget all this and have some fun?"

"You want a cocktail?"

"No! I want a ride on the scenic railway. I've decided it's best to leave coffee and ice-cream until after our tummies have recovered."

He stopped walking and put both his arms around her, whirling her round a couple of times. "A little bit of practice for the rides," he said, releasing her.

She reached up and kissed his cheek. For moments they stared at one another then Patrik pulled her close and before either of them could move or say anything at all, their lips met in a long, tender kiss. When it ended, they remained in each other's arms and Bonnie wished this moment could last for ever. But they broke apart, laughing, as a passing gang of lads gave loud wolf-whistles. The pleasure park gates were ahead of them now.

"This will be my first ride on the scenic railway," Patrik said, taking out his wallet.

"And my first ride this season. I know it's a busman's holiday for you, but at least we can keep away from the Waltzer. And I can do with a good scream after seeing you know who!"

"What is this busman's holiday?"

"I'll explain later. Come on, there's a car just pulling in."

They paid then hurried up the wooden steps to the platform. The front seat of the car was vacant so Patrik held the safety rail back for Bonnie to clamber in. They sat close together while more riders got on, then they were off, the car lumbering towards the steep slope where Bonnie knew, as they were right at the front, they would hover, poised for the drop, until pressure from the rear of the car pushed them over the edge. Below, children were riding roundabouts, people were shading their eyes to watch the scenic railway riders swoop down that first scary slope, and everywhere Bonnie looked, people were enjoying themselves.

Her scream joined many others. Beside her, Patrick had one arm firmly round her waist while he grasped the safety rail with the other. Bonnie's hair streamed behind her and at the bottom, the car whipped round a bend then went up again and down again, the motion throwing them from side to side. It was impossible to hear each other over the rattling and clattering, but Bonnie forgot everything except the thrill of the dives and swerves of the roller coaster until they slowed, cruising smoothly back to the platform.

"I swear I have left my stomach behind," Patrik said solemnly as they got out.

"Did you enjoy it?"

"Very much and I didn't scream once." He took her hand as they headed for the steps leading down. "What next?"

"A quiet one. Are you feeling brave?"

"Of course."

"Then let's have a go on the Ghost Train and see who screams first this time."

CHAPTER 20

Bonnie was downstairs ahead of her mother next morning. The night before, she'd come home to find Diane chatting to guests in the lounge, so after a quick goodnight went off to bed with nothing said about Patrik's situation. To her relief, Mr Hamilton hadn't yet returned but Diane said she was happy to wait up for him, declaring he was never inconsiderate. Bonnie had scampered upstairs, deciding not to reveal details of her chat with Sam until she could sit her mum down and explain her decision.

Bonnie began preparing morning tea trays, trying not to worry about Kay and how her evening had gone with Jack. She couldn't imagine working in silence with her friend, but their row had left a nasty taste in her mouth and she glanced at the clock, wondering how her friend would deal with the situation when she arrived. She didn't have long to wait.

Kay let herself in through the back door. Bonnie was pouring boiling water so concentrated on the job in hand. She heard Kay close the door then clear her throat.

"Bonnie, I'm sorry I was so nasty to you. I realise now how right you were."

Bonnie replaced the kettle on the hob and went over to her friend, giving her a hug. "I'm sorry too. I hate falling out with you. But are you alright?"

"I'm fine. Jack didn't exactly behave well at first, but I told him to clear off if he wasn't capable of spending a quiet evening with me."

"Good for you. Did he leave?"

Kay smiled. "No, thank goodness. He apologised and we talked for ages. I'll tell you all about it some time, but not just now. How did your date go?"

"We had lots of fun plus time to talk properly for once. I've got things to tell you too, but I haven't had a chance to tell Mum yet, so please bear with me until the three of us are on our own."

Diane appeared in the doorway. Bonnie noticed her glancing at the morning tea trays. "Just about to deliver these," she said.

"I'll help you as I'm a bit earlier than usual." Kay was putting her things away.

"Thanks, Kay." Bonnie turned to her mother. "Mum, I need to talk to you when we have our break. This affects Kay too, so I'd like you both to listen to what I have to say."

Bonnie knew full well how fast time passed between morning teas and breakfast. Most holidaymakers didn't want to hang around in the mornings, unless the weather caused them to rethink their plans. Charlie Hamilton followed his usual routine but he as good as grunted a reluctant 'good morning' to her and she was relieved she'd asked Kay to serve him breakfast.

She couldn't wait to sit down with her mum and her friend and explain where she'd gone yesterday afternoon. By the time the morning clearing away was accomplished, she was too excited to eat much, so, between nibbles of buttered toast, she revealed how she'd offered to help Sam out, almost without thinking it through first.

"I've been wondering when you'd begin job

hunting." Diane smiled at her daughter. "And I'm pleased you're going to help Sam while you look for something permanent. He's always been a good friend to us. Well done, Bonnie."

"Kay? What do you think? I shan't go leaving you in the lurch. I'll wait until Mum takes on someone else."

"I'm sure that won't be a problem." Diane interrupted. "Bridget next door is always happy to help out and it's only for a few weeks. At least we know where we are now."

"We all get on well with Bridget," Kay said. "But I wonder if you could ask Mr Booker if I can apply for the permanent job in his office. I know you want something with more prospects, but working for him would suit me very well."

Bonnie gave a slow, surprised whistle. "I thought you said you never wanted to look a typewriter in the face once you finished your secretarial course. What's changed your mind?"

"Maybe I'm learning sense at last. I enjoy working with figures and I'm sure I can brush up my shorthand and typing. Will you put a word in for me, please?"

"Of course. Sam's bound to offer an interview and the rest is up to you. And, Mum, I spoke to Patrik about doing some maintenance work here and he said he'd be honoured to help"

"I thought you were looking starry-eyed this morning." Diane winked at Kay. "Don't tell me you've fixed a job for him with Sam too?"

"I didn't like to say anything, knowing he was about to interview two applicants." She hesitated then locked gazes with her mother. "But I'm afraid there have been things going on, involving Patrik doing some 'moonlighting' – if that's the right word - for Mr Hamilton, Mum." She hesitated. "I think I might have upset Charlie – upset him enough for him to take his business to some other guest house." Bonnie held her breath.

Kay was concentrating on the view through the window. Diane, face expressionless, picked up her teacup and sipped from it as though Bonnie had just asked if any shopping needed doing.

"Mum? Has he said anything to you?"

"No, but I'm intrigued as to what he's done to upset you." Suddenly she gasped. "Oh, Bonnie, please don't tell me he made a pass at you!"

"No! No of course he hasn't! I'd probably have slapped his face if he had, model guest or not."

"Quite right too. Go on then."

"It's a long story. I don't like the way he's been treating Patrik. It started with Mr Hamilton buying him a meal and offering to help him earn more money and better himself. Of course, Patrik was interested – you can imagine how poor he is and he's stuck in a caravan with three other workers. Anyway, Mr Hamilton seems to expect him to jump when he clicks his fingers and rearrange his shifts on the Waltzer with hardly any notice. At first, Patrik was glad of the chance to earn extra cash, but it wasn't long before he suspected things weren't quite as they should be."

"I had no idea this was going on. What kind of things do you mean, love?"

"Mr Hamilton's operating some kind of business that involves collecting goods from the docks or the airport, usually late in the day. He has contacts amongst the employees and each time Patrik's been called out, it's been at a time when there's not much else happening. But on the last occasion, Patrik went to the airport with him and something about Mr Hamilton's attitude made him wonder whether false documentation was being used to get goods through Customs."

Bonnie noticed her mother's expression and wondered whether she'd done right to include Kay in the conversation. This must be worrying for Diane, but she could hardly send her friend out of the room now.

"I can't believe Charlie would break the law. And it sounds as though there's more than one employee involved too. How did Patrik get to know him, anyway? How long has he been working for him?" Diane's hands were clasped beneath her chin, gaze fixed on her daughter.

"Patrik walked me home from the pleasure park the night he and I met near the Waltzer." Bonnie glanced at Kay.

"That's right, Mrs Morgan. It was the same night Jack and I got back together. Jack offered me a lift on the back of his motorbike but I didn't want Bonnie walking all the way back on her own. Patrik offered to escort her."

"And how has this business suddenly come to light? I'm not happy about what I hear. What proof does Patrik have? Could he be imagining things?"

"I'm sorry, Mum. I probably should've said something before, but Patrik wasn't totally certain there might be shady goings on until that last airport trip when the documentation seemed to be on Mr Hamilton's mind. Then when he asked Patrik to give up his funfair job and work solely for him, Patrik felt he might be getting in too deep if he didn't stand up for himself. Mr Hamilton seems to run this extra business alongside his normal sales rep job."

"Oh, my goodness." Diane rose and walked over to the window where she stood, gazing at the garden. "Did you mention any of this to Sam?"

There seemed no point in denying it. "Yes, because I

needed to talk to someone not too close to home."

Diane whirled around. "Did you indeed? And what happens next?"

Bonnie met her mother's gaze. "I've no idea what Mr Hamilton might do. That's why I warned you I'd upset him. I know as well as you do that Sam's absolutely solid gold."

She saw her mother's eyelashes flutter and her mouth tremble just a tad. "This has been a strange season so far, girls. Our takings are on target to be the best ever. I didn't even suffer too much loss when that couple left without paying their bill. You've each found yourself a boyfriend. I've totally misjudged Charlie's character and ... and now it seems Sam's suddenly taking an interest in our lives. I'm so confused."

Bonnie looked down at her nails. Kay stared at the calendar with its picture of a golden cornfield.

"Sam's honest and dependable, but he can't work miracles. Are you telling me I could have the police turning up here, looking for Charlie? He went off this morning as usual, saying he'd see me later."

"I don't know what happens next, Mum. It's Patrik's word against Mr Hamilton's. Sam thinks he knows one of the other people involved but as far as Mr Hamilton's activities are concerned, he only knows what I've heard from Patrik." Bonnie didn't want to hurt her mother any more than necessary. But if Diane asked, she or Kay, would be bound to tell her about Charlie's track record with lady friends.

"What a mess. I did wonder why Charlie chose to base himself here over the summer." She sat down at the table again. "Quite obviously it had nothing to do with his relationship with me – such as it is."

"When he invited you to that dinner dance without much notice, you said you thought he'd probably been turned down by someone else." Bonnie reached over to grasp her mum's hand.

"I did, didn't I? Even at my age, it's nice to be flattered now and then, even if I'm low on his list of favourite females."

Bonnie longed to confide what she suspected Sam felt about her, but didn't dare, in case she jinxed proceedings. It was up to Sam to tell her mother.

"If Patrik's suspicions are correct, I wonder how much longer Charlie can go on operating this illegal venture of his? Should I give him his marching orders? And if I do, what reason could I possibly offer? Just how dangerous do you – or does Patrik – think he is?"

Bonnie sighed. "It's not an easy situation. I'm terrified Patrik might be incriminated because he's accepted money for helping on jobs. But when he accepted the work, he had absolutely no idea he was getting involved with anything crooked."

Diane nodded. "That's understandable. I feel furious when I think of how I've always trusted Charlie – considered him to be the ideal guest – looked forward to his visits." She groaned. "But if the police come knocking on the door, I'm now in a difficult position because I too have been made aware of wrongdoing."

"Oh, my goodness, Mum! I truly didn't think of that. It's not just Patrik and me with suspicions. I told Sam yesterday and now you and Kay both know. This is awful."

"I can't go to the police with an accusation based on hearsay, but in the meantime, it strikes me your boyfriend needs a good solicitor, Bonnie. I have a horrible feeling Patrik's going to need all the help he can get.

CHAPTER 21

"She took it very well, considering what a bombshell I dropped!" Bonnie was sitting opposite Sam again, this time armed with notebook, pens, pencils and typing eraser. He'd already dictated a couple of urgent letters, but was unable to resist asking about Diane.

"It'll be interesting to see what Hamilton does next," Sam said. "I don't mind telling you I don't like the current situation."

"Mum thinks Patrik needs a solicitor's advice. What do you think?"

"I think she's right. Is Patrik working at the funfair today?"

"Yes, after I finish here, I want to go down to the Waltzer to let him know about tomorrow. I won't mention getting legal advice because I know he doesn't have the money to pay for it. Maybe there's a way of finding how to go about getting help?"

"I have one idea. What say I come for a chat with your mum later, then you and I'll drive down to the pleasure park and you can introduce me to your young man?"

"Well, yes, that'd be good, but why do you want to meet him?"

"Because, from what you've told me about Hamilton, I wouldn't put it past him to turn up at

Patrik's caravan and threaten him again. But with greater menace this time. Hamilton won't want his nice little earner interfered with in any way. I'm not trying to frighten you, but I'd be happier if Patrik stayed with me for the next few nights while we sort things out. You know my son's away just now?"

"Fruit picking, isn't he?"

"That's right. The spare room's a mess but Patrik can have my son's bedroom. He needs to come with us as soon as he finishes work tonight, because we daren't risk him going back to the caravan. Make sure he fully understands what I've told you and tell him I'll lend him pyjamas and toiletries."

Bonnie nodded. "I will. Thanks, Sam. It's much appreciated."

"I'll let you get on with typing my letters now. It's at times like this we realise how much we value our dearest friends. The post goes both ways, Bonnie. You've dropped everything to come and organise my office and the least I can do is help your boyfriend out of a jam." He shook his head. "I don't want to frighten you, but it seems to me, the sooner Patrik gets out of Hamilton's clutches, the better it'll be for him."

Patrik was finding it difficult to concentrate. Not only did he find it impossible not to keep thinking of the ride he and Bonnie took on the ghost train the evening before, but he half-expected Charlie to turn up and confront him. Luckily, his conscientious nature made him focus on ensuring riders were safe and happy. To his relief, the businessman still hadn't made an appearance when he spotted Bonnie standing not far from the Waltzer. As soon as he could spare two minutes, he hurried across, unable to prevent a huge smile of delight at seeing her.

"No nightmares after the ghost train?" He planted a quick kiss on her cheek, chuckling delightedly as she blushed a delicate pink.

In the interests of keeping her from becoming too frightened, Patrik had cuddled her and stolen more than one kiss while their car trundled them past scenery where monsters and spooks leered at them and blood-curdling cackles echoed in their ears.

Bonnie had roared with laughter when Patrik almost shot up two feet above their seat as what he later described as cold, sausage-like fingers curled around the back of his neck. Bonnie had been spooked when a giant long-legged spider suspended on a string brushed her face, but they were having fun and Patrik wouldn't have cared if the ride had gone on longer. As the car pushed through the final doors inscribed with the chilling words *The End is Nigh*, he removed his arm from around Bonnie, suddenly reluctant to share his feelings for her with strangers queuing for the ride.

Now she was here to see him again but the expression on her face made him fearful. Was she having second thoughts about their relationship? If so, could he really blame her for not wanting to be involved with someone whose history was so troubled? Patrik's throat tightened as she gazed up at him, her blue eyes concerned. But what she said made no sense at all.

"Patrik, are you prepared to trust me?"

He blinked hard. "Trust you? I think the world of you, Bonnie. Why would I not trust you?"

Her expression softened. "Well, rightly or wrongly, I've taken it upon myself to act on your behalf. At the office today, I confided in Sam Booker and he's offered you accommodation to get you away from the caravan and from you know who."

"I don't ... don't understand. Why is he saying he

will have me to stay when he's never met me?"

"Because, he has a bad feeling about the position you're in and he's a kind, generous man who wants to help. At least for now, you'll have a bedroom of your own. And Sam's promised to keep an eye out for any jobs that might suit you. Please say you'll come with us as soon as you finish work, Patrik. Sam thinks Charlie might turn up at the caravan and I can't bear to think you might be in danger."

Those blue eyes were beseeching now. Their owner hadn't come to tell him she no longer wished to see him. What's more, she was bringing him hope, not only for now but for the future.

"I can defend myself against Hamilton if he tries any rough stuff, but what I fear is him telling lies about me so I lose my job and my place in the caravan. But now your friend is offering me a lifeline. Mr Booker sounds an excellent man. Here I am, a stranger – a foreigner in his land – yet he holds out the hand of friendship. I have you to thank for this, Bonnie."

She squeezed his fingers. "Just leave it all to him and don't be too disappointed if it takes him a while to find a job for you. He's a kind man and he's happy to have you stay with him while things are sorted out. He knows you want to earn more money so you can complete your training.

"Sam's always been there in the background, while my father was away at sea, then after Dad lost his life. Sometimes I wonder whether Sam and Mum might, you know, get together, as they're both widowed. But then she seemed to fall under Charlie Hamilton's spell, though thank goodness she realises now what he's like. I never thought I'd hear myself saying it, but I think Sam's right to worry about your safety."

Patrik turned his head, hearing his name being

called. "I have to go now. I finish at ten o'clock, so you wish me to wait for you to come?"

"Yes. No need to go back to the caravan. Sam will lend you anything you need. See you later, Patrik."

She hurried off through the crowds and Patrik jogged back to the Waltzer. His boss wanted to take a tea break and ordered his employee not to leave the ride under any circumstances.

"One more minute," the boss said before walking away.

"Yes, sir. You can rely on me." Patrik counted up to sixty then pulled the lever to slow the ride. The machinery whirred and hummed as the cars slowed to a halt. Yet another crowd of eager riders had paid good money to be flung around like dolls inside a washing machine.

Bonnie had a few minutes before she met Kay at the ice-cream parlour, giving her an excuse to linger. She saw Patrik holding his hand out to help a little girl jump from the car while her parents waited to follow her. She saw him smile and say something which made them all laugh. Like a lightning bolt, it dawned on her how much she loved this young man and wanted him to realise his potential. If she couldn't find the job she wanted, she'd take any job she could find and continue helping her mum when necessary. Somehow, they'd find a way.

Charlie Hamilton was in his lockup premises, selecting the packages he needed to load into his car. The small black Morris was parked outside, boot open. He was working alone that evening. Ken was almost off the radar. Fair play, the man had been a loyal helper and no way would he spill the beans and incriminate the man who'd provided him with a good little earner over the last few years. Why would he, when that'd mean dropping himself into the mire at the same time?

Charlie was preparing to deliver this consignment to the city where a certain jeweller would let him in through the rear entrance to his shop and Charlie would accept the agreed amount of cash and drive back. On his return he'd give Patrik Matyaz a surprise visit. Frighten the daylights out of him and tell him he needed him tomorrow evening, no messing about. The young Hungarian needed teaching a lesson in politeness and commitment and Charlie would make sure he got it. That was the plan.

Or was it? More and more these days he was returning to a well-worn day dream. A dream in which he settled his affairs and moved abroad to live. In his mind he pictured himself strolling into his favourite bar on the Costa Brava. Maybe tomorrow he'd begin to form a serious plan of action. But there were still deals to be done. Goods to be manipulated.

He was reaching for his jacket when a shadow fell across the open doorway. Damn it! He was slipping – though he'd checked outside to make sure no one was hanging about. But there was nothing here to incriminate him. Everything was neatly packed in cardboard crisp boxes or cartons marked 'Balloons' or 'Glove Puppets.' Charlie shrugged his shoulders into his navy-blue suit jacket, took his car keys from his pocket and strode to the open door of the lock up, pulling it shut behind him and turning the key in the padlock.

Only then did he turn and face the tall man in the nondescript check shirt and khaki trousers who stood waiting for him.

"All right old son? Who are you looking for?" His heart was beating faster than normal, but Charlie pasted a confident smile upon his face and looked his visitor in the eye.

"I spotted you as I walked past. Truth is, I got the sack today, so thought I'd see if there was a job going on the fairground. I don't suppose you need anyone for the rest of the season?"

Charlie felt weak with relief. He'd been half-expecting this bloke to show his ID and explain he was a plain clothes detective. He held out his hand to the visitor. "I'm afraid I can't help you, mate, but I wish you luck."

The man nodded, a gloomy look on his face, and set off, leaving Charlie to lean against the door, heaving a sigh of relief. He was losing it. Definitely losing his appetite for dangerous dealing. He'd begin planning his new life as soon as he got back *to Sea Breezes.* And he'd ask Diane whether she fancied throwing in her lot with him. She could follow him to the Costa Brava once she'd sold her guest house. Maybe they could buy a similar business in Spain. That'd serve her bossy daughter and her precious boyfriend right!

He checked his watch and got into the car. With a bit of luck, he could deliver the goods and return to the pleasure park in time to give that young Hungarian something to think about. No way was he going to let Patrik Matyaz off the hook!

CHAPTER 22

"I reckon we deserve a Knickerbocker Glory. Yum!" Kay raised her long silver spoon, ready to attack the multicoloured tower of vanilla ice cream, fruit and whipped cream tempting her.

"Too right! We've both had a lot on our minds, including me worrying Mum might have been considering teaming up with Mr Hamilton." Bonnie shuddered.

"At least she knows what he's like now."

"She does, and between you and me, I think Sam Booker's ready to ask her out – at long last!"

Kay smiled dreamily. "Maybe love is in the air all around …"

Bonnie took a spoonful of ice cream. "Which reminds me – what did you want to tell me about Jack? I didn't like to ask you before."

"You were right about him. That night he came to my house, he thought he could coax me into doing something I didn't want to do. I got cross and told him to get lost!"

"Good for you. But I'm surprised he doesn't know you better than that."

"I said as much to him. Then, to give him his due, he apologised and we had a lovely evening, cuddled up on the sofa with Pat Boone. But wait for it! He's asked me to consider announcing our engagement at Christmas."

"You and Jack? Engaged?"

"No, me and Pat Boone, of course!" Kay put down her spoon, her eyes shining. "You're probably thinking we're rushing things, but we both know we need more time before we actually get married. It's what I've dreamed of for a while now and it seems Jack feels the same. He's going to try and get a permanent job too. I hope you're happy for me, Bonnie."

"How could I not be? It sounds as though you've both got your feet on the ground."

Bonnie wondered whether Jack had confessed about his previous girlfriend though no way did she intend bringing up that subject. She listened to Kay chattering as they demolished their extravagant ice creams, mind half on what her friend was saying while half wondering whether she and Patrik were destined to be together. She told herself it was far too early in their relationship for guessing games. But secretly she hoped one day she'd be the one confiding special news to her best friend.

"I'd better walk back now, Kay," Bonnie checked her watch. "I want to be home in good time so I can go with Sam and introduce him to Patrik."

They were still chatting as they left the ice-cream parlour. "Hope all goes well for you both," Kay called as she waved goodbye.

"Thanks, Kay. I'm sure it will." Bonnie smiled to herself, seeing her friend give a little skip as she set off.

At half-past nine, as Bonnie and George were about to set off for the fairground, the concourse was still full of people. Coaches had transported scores of people from the Rhondda Valley and other places and Patrik had smiled to himself more than once on hearing the different accents. He always enjoyed talking to these day-trippers, especially listening to the Welsh voices and thinking how musical they were. Bonnie's accent, and that of her friends, was different, even though Golden Sands was not a million miles away from the valleys.

He was saying goodbye to a group of teenagers who'd wanted to know what his nationality was when he noticed a tall figure standing beside the hoopla stall. Patrik felt as though his heart had plummeted to his boots, but as soon as he could, he strode across to speak to his unwelcome visitor.

"I thought I made it clear I was not happy to work for you, Mr Hamilton."

Charlie sniggered. "I must've been mistaken when I took you as having a good brain, old son. Why look a gift horse in the mouth?"

Patrik hadn't a clue what he meant about the horse but the rest of the comment stung. He mustn't get angry. Bonnie and her good friend would arrive soon and he didn't want them dragged into any unpleasantness. He sucked in air, hoping to calm his racing heartbeat.

"Look, I'm doing you a favour, Patrik. Between you and me, I've decided to close down my business by the end of the season. This is your last chance to help me out so don't mess with me. If you do, I'm warning you, it'll be the downfall of you. I'll tip off that boss of yours and he'll have you out of your job and that manky caravan before you can say Jack Robinson! You better believe it ..."

Patrik swallowed hard. He moved closer to Charlie, standing toe to toe, the voice of Patti Page singing *The Tennessee Waltz* ringing in his ears as the music rippled through the loudspeaker system. Those words were so poignant. He didn't want to lose Bonnie. If he was aggressive with Charlie and someone called the police, he could end up in prison. He'd be disgraced before he'd even taken up Mr Booker's kind offer of help.

Charlie was gripping the tops of Patrik's arms now. The older man's eyes blazed, his expression surprising Patrik with its intensity.

"I need you tomorrow night. I shan't say this again, Patrik, but if you're not ready when I collect you from the caravan at nine o'clock, it'll be the worse for you. Get it?"

Still Patrik kept his cool. "Why can you not recruit someone else if you're so anxious to get another job done? I've told you already. I don't want to know and I have other plans now."

"Other plans?" Charlie snorted. "Like what, mate? Helping do the washing back at Sea Breezes?"

Patrik's ability to stay calm was being sorely tested. He tried to wrench his arms from Charlie's grasp. Caught unawares, Charlie stumbled and fell against the side of the hoopla stall. But Patrik's attention was elsewhere. He'd glanced across to the Waltzer and noticed something amiss. He gasped as he realised the implications of what was happening. The awful possibility of what could happen while he wrangled with the desperate businessman.

Patrik leapt into action. Hurling himself towards the Waltzer. Shouting out to his boss to stop the ride he'd just set in motion. Unseen by anybody else, a small girl who must have wandered away from her parents, had climbed up on to the wooden platform and wriggled her way through the cars so she now sat on one of the metal struts joining the cars to the central hub. The ride was progressing slowly now. Lulling riders before the machinery revved up to take those riders into the relentless swinging and lurching so characteristic of the

Spanish Waltzer.

The singer was bemoaning the loss of her little darlin' and Patrik knew he was the only person who could save this particular little girl - someone's much-loved daughter – from a terrifying ordeal. She might be perfectly safe if she remained sitting on the ground while the cars whirled above her head. But what if she became frightened and tried to climb back up? Quickly, he clambered down and reached for the child, scooping her up in his arms. She began to cry.

"It's all right, baby," he crooned. By now he was balancing on one of the struts. He had moments before the cars began to move faster. Hardly any of them were occupied. He shouted again. But his boss had disappeared inside the booth and the music boomed and echoed in Patrik's ears. His only chance was the third car along which he could see was occupied by a man and woman.

Patrik shouted to them. "Be ready to take her from me. And try to get the ride stopped." He locked gazes with the very startled male rider and held out the little girl so the stranger could take her into the car.

"I've got her!"

Patrik felt weak with relief as he heard people shouting for help. Someone was heading for the kiosk to alert the ride's proprietor. Patrik lowered himself so he was sitting astride the steel strut. He hung on. Didn't the English call this hanging on for grim death? He was losing his balance. The mechanism hadn't yet kicked in to slow down the ride. Patrik lost his hold. As he fell to the ground, he banged his head on the huge metal component designed to underpin the whole apparatus so it operated safely.

The little girl was out of harm's way. That was his last thought as he sank into darkness.

CHAPTER 23

Charlie was in a world of his own. He didn't wait to check what Patrik was up to, but recovered his balance and set off for his car. Fine! He'd just have to do this job by himself. It would take him longer, but it was the final consignment arriving by sea from the Italian company he'd dealt with for years.

His contact at the docks was retiring, which fitted in with Charlie's plan to close down his extra business. He'd had high hopes of Patrik Matyaz but the boy wasn't playing ball. And what if he talked? Charlie daren't risk that.

He decided to catch Patrik later. He'd return after collecting this final consignment from the docks and if necessary, turn up at the caravan and frighten the young Hungarian into keeping silent and helping him clear up a few projects while Charlie worked out his notice with the firm who employed him as a sales representative. Only then would he be able to make his escape to sunny Spain and an exciting new future.

He'd had a good run. Importing contraband goods wasn't something he'd imagined himself doing and now he had a hefty amount of money in several different bank accounts, it was time to move on. Patrik had let Charlie down badly by not jumping at the chance to earn more money. If he'd only co-operated and done what he was told, Charlie mightn't have been quite so ready to give up his lucrative little side-line.

He crossed the fairground, oblivious to the sights and sounds around him. So intent was he on mentally totting up the profit he anticipated from the sale of tonight's consignment of gold watches, he didn't notice a grey-haired man, dressed casually, following him at a safe distance.

Charlie reached his car, unlocked it and got in. He'd miss his precious Jaguar, but it would have to go. He'd come this far and now he could see the promised land. He started the engine and pulled away, humming *The Tennessee Waltz* as he left the bright lights behind. Later, Patrick would doubtless regret being so rude as to dash away while Charlie was speaking to him.

The plain clothes detective and his sidekick set off the moment the red Jag passed them and turned the corner. They had a rough idea their suspect would be heading either for the dockyard or the airport. They'd also been keeping tabs on a certain jeweller in the city, so that was another option. If information received proved accurate, they could catch Mr Charles Hamilton red-handed.

Keeping a discreet distance behind his vehicle, only side lights on as there was still plenty of daylight left, the driver gave an 'ah' of satisfaction as their quarry took the turning leading to the dockyard. This had all the makings of an easy pinch.

"Don't get too close," the senior officer warned his driver. "We don't want him spotting us and pulling over for a cigarette."

As the unmarked police vehicle lost speed, the red Jaguar turned down a side road.

"Hold on. Let him reach his destination. There's no missing that car so we can bide our time now." The detective opened the glove compartment and took out a packet of peppermints. "There's only one other route out of this part of the docks. And that water's very cold and very deep."

"OK, guv," his colleague said. "Can't wait to see his face when you bid him a good evening!"

Ten minutes later, Charlie Hamilton's dream of sangria and sunshine met an abrupt end as he listened to his rights being read to him.

Sam parked near the fairground. "Amazing sunset," he said. "I'm glad to be seeing it instead of sitting indoors watching the box."

"I expect you need to relax, working as hard as you do," Bonnie said, as they got out of the car.

"Your mother's as bad, if not worse."

Bonnie laughed. "True." She stopped walking. "Look! There's an ambulance coming through the main gates. Gosh, Sam, I hope nothing too dreadful has happened."

"At least whoever's inside is in good hands. Lead the way to the Waltzer then, so we can collect your young man."

"It's not far." Bonnie was glancing around her. Stalls were being closed down for the night and none of the rides were operating. The pungent aroma of fried onions still hung in the air and she could see the Waltzer's gaudy paintwork ahead. She heard a woman say how awful it was that a little girl had got lost and nearly come to grief. Whatever had her parents been thinking of?

Bonnie wondered if the ambulance had been taking the child to hospital and hoped the little one hadn't been badly injured. Suddenly she spotted Jack, standing beside the Waltzer's kiosk. He was looking straight at her. And he wasn't smiling.

She forgot Sam. Forgot she was wearing high-heeled sandals. Forgot everything as she ran forward, narrowly missing knocking into a man pushing a wheelbarrow full of rubbish bags. Jack jumped off the wooden platform and came towards her.

"What's happened? Where's Patrik?"

Jack put an arm around her shoulders. "Come and sit down over there."

"Tell me!"

Jack led her to the nearby bench while Sam, who'd just arrived, made his way on to the ride where its owner was talking to a group of men.

"Patrik's a hero."

Bonnie sucked in her breath. What was going on? "What's happened, Jack? Please tell me he's alive!"

Jack squeezed her hand. "He was unconscious from his fall so they've taken him to hospital. He'll be fine, Bonnie. He's in good hands. Oh, heck, don't cry!"

But the tears streamed down Bonnie's face. She wanted to know how Patrik had been hurt and couldn't bear to think of him suffering and in hospital among strangers. Jack was patting her hand and Sam was hurrying towards them.

Jack got to his feet and Bonnie buried her face in her hands, still sobbing.

Sam bent over her. "I'm going to drive you to the hospital. Do you want to collect your mum on the way?" He produced a large, white handkerchief from his jacket pocket and gently prised her hands loose.

Like an infant, she let him mop her tears. "I ... I'd rather go straight there, please."

"Of course. You can probably help the medical staff by giving them information about Patrik. You take my arm, love. Are you coming too, Jack?"

"Yes, please. If Bonnie doesn't mind."

She shook her head. Was she taking part in a play? She certainly felt as though she was. Somehow, she was walking along, Sam on one side and Jack on the other. She kept seeing her boyfriend's handsome face smiling down on her. He should be here, holding her hand – teasing her as he had over her terrible accent when she tried saying a few words he'd taught her of his own language.

She'd learned how to say "My name is Bonnie" and he'd replied in Hungarian, though refusing to say what it meant. She'd watched his eyes twinkling as he smiled his gorgeous smile and she suspected what he'd said to her, but daren't insist on him translating.

It was as though her brain couldn't accept the awfulness of the situation. She was back in Sam's car. But instead of Patrik in the rear seat, it was Jack asking Sam which hospital they were heading for. And it wasn't the small, local one, but the big one, several miles away. Knowing this made her tremble, and the trembling continued, even though she heard Sam ask Jack to wrap the tartan car rug around her.

Sam and Jack were discussing how brave Patrik had been, back at the funfair, their voices low as though they were afraid to disturb her. All she could think of was whether Patrik would pull through. What if he ... she swallowed hard as the frightening possibility gnawed at her. What if Patrik never woke up again?

CHAPTER 24

Holding Sam's arm, Bonnie followed Jack up the stairs to the next floor. Both of them had been so kind, Sam especially. Her mum would say she'd expect nothing less of him. She'd also say not even Sam could work miracles. Nobody could. But Bonnie was desperately hoping for a miracle that evening.

She prayed the young Hungarian would recover consciousness, having received a heavy, potentially damaging, blow to his head. After all he'd gone through whilst fleeing his home country and arriving in a strange, new world, she couldn't bear the thought of his life being cut short, especially after such an act of bravery.

Sam had told her Patrik's youth and strong constitution were positive factors. Jack had chimed in, saying how many of the fairground workers were holding him in their thoughts. Willing him to recover. Bonnie had gone beyond tears now. All she felt was the strange sense of unreality that had hit her earlier.

All at once, Jack was pushing through the swing doors. She breathed in the hospital smell. Sam propelled her towards another doorway, where she leet go of his arm and took a deep breath.

"Are you OK?"

"Yes. I'm praying hard, Sam."

"That's the ticket. I think we're all sending up prayers." Sam approached the staff nurse. The young woman looked up and smiled, obviously recognising him.

"Hello, Mr Booker. How can I help?"

"Dr Collins has given Miss Morgan here, permission to see Patrik Matyaz. I hope that's possible?" His words hung on the air.

The nurse's face remained neutral. "Of course. Could I take some details from you first, Miss Morgan?"

Bonnie swayed a little and Jack took her arm and whispered to her that everything was going to be alright. She answered the questions, still feeling as though she was an outsider looking in at some drama or other. When she stated the name of Patrik's next of kin, Sam remembered he had Istvan's phone number in his pocket book and read it out to the nurse.

Staff Nurse then led Bonnie down a corridor and into a private room. And at last, there was Patrik. So still. So pale. His dark hair tousled; he lay beneath a blue blanket. Another nurse stood at the foot of his bed, writing something on a chart.

Bonnie couldn't take her eyes off Patrik. His jet-black eyelashes made little fans against his cheeks. The dark stubble on his chin made him, she thought, look even more handsome. But he remained motionless, apart from the gentle rise and fall of his breathing.

"If Mr Matyaz doesn't regain consciousness soon, we'll need to sedate him while further treatment is carried out." The Ward Sister had entered the room and now gave Bonnie a sympathetic look. "On the other hand, the signs indicate your friend could return to consciousness any time. Why don't you hold his hand and try speaking to him?"

Someone pulled forward a chair and Bonnie sank

into it. She reached for Patrik's hand and gave it a gentle squeeze. Where should she start?

He was moving. That's all he knew. Suddenly he was in the rowing boat with his mother, father and brother. The sun shone from a cloudless blue sky – that special shade of blue – reminding him of the flowers growing wild around his grandparents' country home. His father was guiding the boat towards a little landing stage, a favourite place to moor and eat lunch on the river bank.

Istvan was telling one of his terrible jokes. An extremely silly joke that made everybody groan. Patrik punched his brother on the arm and Istvan punched him back. Gently. Their mother warned them not to rock the boat, insisting they could swim back if they didn't behave. He knew she didn't really mean it.

He felt peaceful. Yet something – or someone – was missing from this idyllic scene. A girl ... of course, that was who was absent. A beautiful girl with hair like golden silk. He was looking for her, wondering if she'd appear from the nearby woodland and call his name. He strained to hear her. Surely, she must be nearby?

Now his family had disappeared, leaving him on his own. No more blue sky and sunshine – just a hazy mist he struggled to escape from, but without success. He could hear someone calling his name now. Why couldn't he respond? Where was he? He wanted to open his eyes and see who was holding his hand. But he couldn't seem to manage it.

Now whoever bent over him wore a perfume he knew from somewhere. Such a sweet, floral scent ... Again, Patrik tried to open his eyes.

"I'm sure his eyelids twitched just then." Bonnie looked across at Sister.

"Excellent. Squeeze his hand. See if he responds."

Bonnie swallowed the enormous boulder in her throat and gently squeezed Patrik's fingers. Her breath snagged in her throat. Her tears were back and streaming down her cheeks. She hardly dared breathe. Dare not move in case she startled him. Because the young Hungarian was gripping her fingers as though he never wanted to let her go.

She stroked his cheek with her other hand. Behind her, someone entered the room. An older, bearded version of Patrik walked round to the opposite side of the bed and nodded at her, his expression solemn and his anguish showing in his eyes. "You are Bonnie?"

"Yes. And you must be Istvan. I'm pleased they managed to contact you."

She looked down at Patrik. His eyelids were definitely twitching. They were making his dark eyelashes flutter, like butterfly wings.

"Patrik? Darling Patrik, can you hear me?" Relief rushed through Bonnie as she felt him squeeze her fingers for a second time.

Istvan walked around the bed to stand beside her. Slowly ... very slowly ... the patient moved his head so he faced both of them.

"Say something to us, little brother." Istvan whispered something in his own language and smoothed Patrik's hair so tenderly, tears welled again in Bonnie's eyes. Sister moved forward and handed her a white handkerchief so she could mop up her tears.

The room was quiet, but when Patrik opened his eyes and looked at Bonnie, she had no idea what he was saying.

She turned to Istvan. "Can you translate for me, please?"

"He said *I love you* and I don't think he was talking to me."

Bonnie laughed with relief but most of all with joy. "Please say it in Hungarian for me, so I can say it straight back to him."

When she repeated Istvan's words, Patrik smiled then closed his eyes again.

Bonnie froze, but Sister moved swiftly forward to check his pulse. "He'll probably fall into a natural sleep now. But he's on the mend. Our hero will be blushing once he fully wakes and realises how much interest there's been in him. We've already had BBC local radio on the phone."

A few days after Patrik moved into Sam's house and the doctor pronounced him fit enough to go out on his own, he walked round to Sea Breezes where he received a huge hug from Bonnie's mum. The afternoon was warm and sunny, so Bonnie took glasses of homemade lemonade into the garden, feeling almost shy as she sat down beside Patrick.

What he said at the hospital after regaining consciousness might simply have been prompted by relief. She still felt too raw to mention it.

Besides, Patrik and Sam had been plotting – or so Sam had told Diane. There had also been something of great interest in the local paper, quite apart from a glowing report headed *Young Hungarian fairground worker saves little girl's life!*

"Thank you." Patrik raised his glass and chinked it against hers. "Here's to the future."

"It's looking good for you, Patrik." Bonnie sipped her lemonade. "Have you seen the local paper yet?"

"Sam read out the piece about Mr Hamilton being kept in, um ... custody? He asked his solicitor whether I should come forward to make a statement, so I told them everything."

"It's such a relief it's all over. Did you also see the piece about you rescuing that small girl?"

"Yes, but anyone would have done the same."

"I'm not so sure about that, but I shan't argue. When you rang from Sam's, you promised to tell me what all this plotting and planning's been about."

He reached for her hand. "It is very exciting. Istvan found someone to take over my job on the Waltzer, but Sam has made ... um, suggestion. He says, if I redecorate his spare room, I can have it for as long as I want to stay. His son will use his old bedroom before he goes off to university."

"That's marvellous! Has Sam found any job vacancies that might suit you?"

"Not yet, but I shall keep trying and Sam will charge me nothing so I will repay him by helping with gardening and house jobs. Best of all, he has contacted the technical college and told them about me. They wish to see me, because one or two peoples have dropped out of the ... ophthalmological course and I am halfway through my studies, so I could join the second-year students."

Bonnie swallowed hard. "I'm so proud of you, Patrik."

"All this has happened because fate brought me into your path, lovely Bonnie."

"What, you mean when I almost knocked you over?"

He laughed, put his arms around her and gently tilted her face towards his. "I have not known you for long, but long enough to know I never want to let you go from my life. I cannot offer you anything yet, only my promise to love you and look after you for the rest of our lives."

"I ... I don't know what to say." Bonnie couldn't believe her dreams were coming true.

"In the hospital, when I say to you, *I love you*, I meant every word – even if you needed to ask my brother to explain this to you."

He was teasing her! "Well, I love you too." She managed to repeat the words she'd memorised and which she whispered every night before she went to sleep, to make sure she didn't forget them.

He tried to kiss her, just as she snuggled closer. They bumped noses, then both burst out laughing. But as he took her in his arms and she closed her eyes, Bonnie lost herself in their deep yet tender kiss.

However long it might take, one day she and Patrik would make a home together and build a family. She intended to spend the rest of her life, loving her handsome Hungarian.

The End

ABOUT THE AUTHOR

Jill Barry is a multi-published author of contemporary and historical novels who enjoys nothing better than creating problems and pitfalls for her main characters. She isn't afraid to tackle difficult issues, but often beguiles her readers with touches of gentle humour.

You'll find Jill's contemporary and historical romances at www.jillbarry.com and available via all leading online book suppliers, also those on your High Street.

Jill also writes Pocket Novels for D C Thomson and her Linford Romances are available through the public library system.

Printed in Great Britain
by Amazon